No More Miss B. Havin

by

Lydia M. Lacy

P. O. Box 24374
Detroit, MI 48224
(866) 882-1159
www.gpublishingsuccess.com

This book is a work of fiction. Places, events, and situations in this story are purely fictional and any resemblance to actual persons, living or dead, is coincidental.

Republished by G Publishing 01/10/05
Detroit, Michigan

ISBN: 0-9727582-8-3

Library of Congress Control Number: 2004093639

Printed in the United States of America

This book is printed on acid-free paper.

DEDICATION

Gracious Lord, I truly thank you for giving me the opportunity to write this novel. I know that with you all things are possible. I dedicate this book to all of my family and closest friends. To my loving husband for always supporting me, no matter what. To my two beautiful baby girls, Kamryn and Kourtney, for always making me smile. To my rock, LaToi Patillo for always keeping it real with me. To my girlfriend, Roslyn Fluker, thanks for laughing at me. Mommie, thanks for always telling me the truth about myself and still loving me. A special shout out goes to Marlon Holmes, my good friend from way back. May he rest in peace. I thank my grandparents for keeping me in the church. Thanks, Granny for letting me cry on your shoulder. To my auntie-momma Carolyn for reading my manuscript and always being there for me. To my daddy who gave me sound advice even when I didn't want to hear it. Thanks to all of those who support me by purchasing and reading this book. I LOVE YOU ALL!

KYLE

It was a bright, cool, and sunny October Sunday morning and the pulpit of The Community Christian Fellowship church was full. The choir sang beautifully and the pastor's sermon was once again uplifting. The women in the church had on their fall colored Sunday gear and the men were respectfully noticing each and every one of them. That is with the exception of Kyle. He didn't even notice the women who were admiring him. It had been almost two weeks since Tamara had broken up with him and he hadn't noticed another woman since. Their relationship had been both stressful and draining for him, but their break up was even worse. Depression had set in for a while, but after this morning's service, there were no signs of it.

He listened to the Pastor preach today and felt as though he was speaking directly to him. To Kyle, the message was very clear. It was from Hosea 1:2. It read, *"Go, take unto thee a wife of whoredom and children of whoredom: for the land hath committed great whoredom, departing from the Lord."* God had told Hosea to go in the world and find a worldly woman, marry her, and bare children. Without question, Hosea did as he was told and obeyed the Lord.

Kyle had always felt that he was a loyal servant of the Lord and wondered if being with Tamara is what the Lord wanted for him. He put his head down, closed his eyes and began to pray silently. "Lord, I am tired of being depressed. I know that it is time for me to be a happy man. You have blessed me with so much in the past and I know that you will continue to do so in the future. If Tamara and I are to be together, Father, I ask that you send her back to me. If not, Father, I ask that you help me to move on with my life and bless and watch over my wife, whomever she may be. Keep her safe and out of all harm's way. In Jesus name, Amen." And with that, he let go of Tamara and all of his depression!

When the Pastor asked all of those who were to be baptized to approach the pulpit, he was the first in line. He grabbed the microphone and cleared his throat as the congregation cheered him on.

"Praise him!" "Amen, brother!"

"Amen, and praise him Brother Sinclair. Yes Lord, I've known this man for quite a while. Saints, he's been a member of our church family for about two years now."

Then turning towards the small group dressed in all white robes, the Pastor spoke directly to

Kyle and the others, and said, "Please tell the church members why have you chose to get baptized this morning?"

Kyle swallowed hard and took his time to carefully plan out what he was going to say to the waiting crowd. "Well Pastor, as you know, this year has been a troubling one for me, but the Lord has seen me through it all. I made a promise to him and myself that I would get myself together, and now is the time."

Patting him on the back and giving a half hug, the Pastor took the microphone back into his own hands and said, "Amen! Brother, that is wonderful! Please join Deacon Watts and the others in the back and they will give you further instructions."

As he stepped down from the pulpit, Kyle noticed the puddle of sweat that had settled in the palms of each of his hands. He walked towards the exit sign on the right and down the hall to a small flight of stairs that led to the baptism pool. There was no turning back now. He took another deep breath, swallowed hard, and took his first step to the rest of his life. He was turning every thing over to the Lord. When he reached the top of the stairs, two old women greeted him. One of them hugged him and kissed his face while the other smiled and encouraged him to continue to move forward where two men waited patiently for him to come into the water. One of the gentlemen held his hand out to help Kyle step into the surprisingly warm calm water. He could see the congregation through the glass window and heard the pastor humming an old tune his grandmother, bless her soul, used to sing to him.

There was definitely no turning back, so he moved closer to Deacon Watts, who was already standing knee deep in the pool. He folded his arms across his chest, took a deep breath, and with ease let the men baptize him in the name of Jesus. What seemed like five minutes under the water was actually two seconds, but Kyle really felt as though all of his sins, burdens, fears, and heartache were left in that water when he stepped out on the other side of the pool. He smiled and slowly descended the stairs into the cold and empty basement where he was to dry off and change into his clothes. He knew his parents (who were divorced) were waiting, so he hurried to get to them before they started any scenes that would embarrass him.

He joined the middle aged couple in the sanctuary and heard the Pastor's benediction before the church had let out. His mom hugged and congratulated him while his father stood reserved and greeted his son with a nod of the head. He knew then that words had already passed between the two, but he refused to get into it with either one of them today. He stuck out his hand to his pops and thanked him for coming and when the doors of the church were opened, they all said their goodbyes and went their separate ways.

BIANCA

I was tired. I had worked all day and my feet were swollen. The mall parking lot was full, so I decided to valet my car while I did some last minute shopping for the wedding. The skinny white kid ran up to my door and opened it before I could grab my purse and the Neiman's bag with the shoes I needed to return. "I wish I had half of the energy you have right now," I said mustering a smile. "Don't park too far hun', I'll be right back. I won't be but twenty minutes tops."

"Sure thing Ma'am!"

"Wow! I'm at Ma'am status already," I thought to myself as I opened the doors to the fabulous Somerset mall. Speaking out loud, "O.K. B., in and out. No window shopping today!"

Peaches was getting married and I did not want to be late. Even though I knew this wedding would not start on time, I still needed to hustle to return the shoes, buy a gift, get my nails done, get back home, and then get dressed. I thought about wearing my orange silk shirt dress, but remembered at the last minute that it was still at the cleaners and it wouldn't be ready for pick up until Wednesday, which was four days away. So, the navy blue Jones of New York suit with the light blue blouse would have to make due. But, in order to wear that, I need new navy blue pumps, not the black ones I'd purchased weeks ago.

The return and purchase of the new shoes took an hour, which only left two and a half hours before the start of the wedding. I was going solo so that wouldn't hold me up any, but waiting for the valet attendant to retrieve my car and getting to the nail salon was a whole different story. I tipped the teenager, threw my bag in the trunk, and sped off at raceway speed. At this pace, I knew I'd make it to my two o'clock appointment by two thirty. But just as I was approaching the 8-mile exit off of the I-75 expressway, the state troopers pulled up behind and flagged me down.

I slowed down and put my blinker on to come off at the exit, came to a complete stop, and hit the steering wheel, yelling, "FUCK! I'll never make it to this stupid wedding."

Noticing my frustration as he approached the driver side of the car slowly, the trooper spoke calmly, "Ma'am can I see some I.D., proof of insurance, and a registration to this vehicle?"

I obliged reaching into my purse to give him the requested items. I turned down the radio and began mumbling to myself as the trooper walked back to his squad car. "I should just take my ass home and call it a fucking day. This is going to be a bullshit ass wedding anyway. I don't even know why people go through all of the fucking trouble. I am not ever doing that dumb shit. All these men out here and silly bitches like this just want to be wit' one. What the fuck is that shit about? Man, I am twenty years old and sitting on top of the world. I am black, beautiful, intelligent, young and wild. Sometimes it's hard for me to even believe God put all of this into one neat package, but he did and I am going to enjoy all of this shit."

After about ten minutes of this ranting and raving to myself, the trooper, believing I was half crazy, handed me the driver's license, and the rest of my belongings, gave me a warning, smiled, and let me off with a simple pat on the wrist. Pulling down the visor to check out my looks in the mirror before I sped off again, I smiled and then licked my lips, "Hey, I am the bomb!"

It was my senior year at Wayne State University, and I was carrying a 3.8 grade point average. School was never really a challenge for me, so I went all three semesters every year and was about to receive my bachelor's degree in accounting four months before my 21st birthday.

As far as dating went, this five foot four inch, size 36-28-41, girl had her pick, every month. However, my boyfriend at the time, Chauncey, was never the wiser. We had dated in high school off and on. He was two years my senior and very attractive. I don't like to admit it too often but, I fell in love with him the first time I bumped into him trying to clear the halls during one of Cass Technical High school's infamous hall sweeps. He had the smile that made me surrender to him completely. Unfortunately, about half the girls in his class surrendered, too.

It was during one of our off spells one chick in particular, Kelly Winston, persuaded him to take her to his senior prom. Nine months later, my man, was Kelly's "baby's daddy." Needless to say, I was heartbroken and from then on I vowed to dog his sorry ass.

So, I started dating several men at a time, since the tenth grade. Now I was dating Steve on Friday nights, Darryl on Saturday nights, and Ronnie on Sundays. Steve worked for Chrysler full time and attended Wayne State part time. He had his own apartment, car, and money, which was my favorite part. He took me to nice restaurants and plays at the Fox Theater. He had class, but was very boring.

We met at The Fishbone's Café downtown one afternoon when my cousin, Kisha, and I were having lunch. He was eating alone at the table next to ours and I invited him over to dine with us. He was wearing a Detroit Lions sweatshirt and hat with a pair of nice fitting blue jeans. It was nothing sexy, however, he was still appealing.

Kisha thought it was a terrible idea to include him in our day out, so she would give me dirty looks across the table when he wasn't looking. But, I thought spending time with a woman was a far cry from spending time with a man. Kisha later apologized for her rude behavior when he offered to pay for our meals. He asked me to join him for breakfast the next morning and I accepted. From that point on, he decided he wanted to see me every week.

On Saturdays, when Chauncey thought I had to attend a weekly study group, I would see Darryl. He was a barber who worked at the same hair salon with my girlfriends, Tonya and Peaches. We would go to lunch or dinner, the movies, or to the recreation center at his apartment complex to play pool. He was fine with a capital "F." "Yummy from head to toe." He was six feet four inches tall with a caramel skin tone, hazel eyes, and thick in all the right places. I loved the way he wore his neatly trimmed fade and beard.

We met one Saturday when Tonya was running late. I sat at the shampoo bowl and watched him wash perm from an older gentleman's hair. When he looked up and noticed me, I blew him a kiss and winked my left eye. It took him by surprise and he laughed out loud. "I love a woman who can express her feelings so openly," he said as he helped the man up from the chair and escorted him to his workstation. A few minutes later, he gestured for me to come and sit next to him as he wrapped the nexus strips around the gentleman's head and told his assistant to show him to the overhead dryers.

"Please tell me you are single and waiting for me."

"Why would I do that?"

"Was I wrong to assume that you were winking at me?"

"No!"

"Then you do want me?"

"Yes, very much so. But, I'm not single nor will I ever wait for you."

"What will you do?"

"I can't tell you all my secrets, but I can tell you that you'll enjoy it."

"From a distance you look like a good girl. I can't believe I'm hearing all of this from you."

"I am a good girl. Good at everything I do! Believe dat!"

"Girl, I love you! Let me take you out."

As we exchanged phone numbers, Tonya showed up and that was the end of that conversation. However, over the course of that relationship, Darryl did my hair free of charge every week, and sometimes twice a week. Three months had gone by before Tonya informed me of the latest gossip going around the shop. *"Girl, Darryl has a girlfriend and she is five months pregnant."*

He tried to lie about it for a while by saying *"I'm not even sure if its mine"* and *"we broke up before you and I met."* I played along with Darryl for as long as I could and then decided to cut him off and that was the end of that fling. You see it's not that I was bothered at all by the fact that he had a woman or that she was pregnant. I was more peeved that he would lie about it. I had a man and Darryl was aware of that, I would not have been upset.

I firmly believe that "honesty is the best policy"

when you are fooling around in the dating game. I learned that from a young player who used to sell weed to my roommate, Sarah. His name was Tracey, but around the way, everybody called him the "Big Ol' Pimp." He looked like Notorious B.I.G. and acted like Ice Cube. He had many women and was considered a player because none of them knew about each other. However, Tracey knew everything about them and their extras. He used to say, *"Baby, I tell my women to always be honest with me. If there is another man in the picture, so be it. But I need to know just in case I need to cover my own ass. 'Cause guys are crazy nowadays and I don't want to be out and have to shoot somebody because I'm with dey woman. Shit, just tell me! I won't be mad."*

That was why it was so easy for me to pretend I was Ronnie's cousin when his woman called his house on Sunday nights. We met at a party on a Saturday at the D.A.V. hall on Jefferson. The radio station, WJLB, was having a singles cabaret and the place was packed from wall to wall. I saw him and his boy standing near the bar staring, so I casually approached him.

"Will you dance with me?"

He responded with a cold *"No."*

Anybody who knew me also knew that I was totally surprised by that one. So with plenty of attitude, I said, *"Excuse you! I was doing you a favor by asking you to dance. Please don't act like you wasn't over here staring and wishing you could think of some sweet line you could approach me with!"*

He thought it was cute that I was angry so he apologized and told me, *"I'm flattered that you want to dance with me, but I'd rather do other things with you."*

I was totally surprised one week later when he revealed that he was only 19 years old. He stood at least six feet tall, was dark brown with sexy Tupac eyes, and big sexy lips like L. L. Cool J's. By Tuesday, which was three days later, we had thoroughly enjoyed each other's body and company. When I asked him where he learned to use the candles, body oils, blindfolds, and ice cubes, he replied, *"on HBO."* I wasn't mad at him for lying about his age. How could I be? Homeboy had it going on!

He lived in a house with two of his *real* cousins and they all worked full time jobs with Pepsi. He had his own car and money. Besides being a "baby's daddy" to a three year old little girl, he was a good young man. So, I would politely answer his telephone, *"Hello."*

"Who is this and why are you answering my man's phone?"

"Oh! Hey Sheila? This is Bianca, Ronnie's cousin. He talks about you all the time. How are you?"

"Bianca, uh oh, yeah I'm fine. Thanks for asking. Is Ronnie there?"

"Yeah! Hold on a minute he's in the bathroom. I'll get him for you."

"Oh! That's O.K. just tell him to call me when

he gets a chance, I was paging him and he wasn't returning my calls I was just checking to see if he was at home with some bitch. You know how these men are."

"Yeah, I know girl, cause I have to check on my man sometimes too. I'll tell him to call you. O.K. bye!"

When I hung up the phone the two of us would spend hours laughing at the poor girl. Then we would watch a porno flick from his collection and I would unzip his pants and go to work like the women he loved to watch. When Sheila called back in the mornings I would simply say he had already left for work.

BIANCA

Yeah, I was having a good time and only the jealous type could be mad at me. I got to the salon at two thirty as estimated and Tasha, the nail tech, was handling all of Peaches' clients today. She was mad, but I didn't care. I sat down in the chair, put my cute red Dolce and Gabbana handbag on my lap, took off my coat, and placed my hands on the table. Then I looked Tasha boldly in the eyes and said, *"Ah bitch I'm giving you my money this shit isn't free, stop trippin' I got stopped by the police trying* to *get here on time."*

Smacking her lips and rolling her eyes, Tasha pulled out some cotton balls, soaked them in polish remover, and began to work on my hands. *"You better tell me something, coming up in here like you running thangs. You know I got other clients to get rid of before the wedding. I still got to go home and get dressed myself."*

"Girl ain't nobody else coming up in here for you. I'll drop you off on my way home. You know

this wedding is going to be on CP time anyway. We still got another two hours to kill."

"Eh! You bringing Chancery's fine ass up in there, or what?"

"Or what. Girl, please there are so many single mutherfuckers that show up at wedding receptions. Why would I bring Chauncey's broke ass?"

"Yeah right! If he knew you were out creepin' he'd beat that ass."

"O.K. now I'm really through talking to your silly ass. I'm a grown ass woman and my own daddy doesn't hit me, I wish I might let some dumb ass mutherfucker put his hands on me. I am not married and even if I were, I'd stab a man tryin' to beat me. If he's that mad, he should dump me, but don't fucking hit me. I mean that shit!"

"I hear dat! You know Darryl is bringing his girlfriend tonight. Watch you' back. She's a trip. A real hood rat; she'll fight you wit' her big ass belly and all."

"I am not thinking about Darryl. I'm trying to get me a new dude up in this joint tonight. I hear Peaches' man knows a lot of ballers and please believe I'm trying to roll."

Giving each other a high five, we finished up our gossip and small talk and I was on my way home in an hour. I tied up my hair, jumped in the shower, got dressed, and put my makeup on in under twenty minutes. I looked in the mirror for a final glance over and called out to my roommate, Sarah, for a second opinion. "What do you think?"

Too busy wrapping the wedding present, Sarah gave me a quick peek and nodded her head in approval. "Thanks girl, I really appreciate you wrapping that for me I am running late."

"Yeah right! Even if you were two hours early, you still would have asked me to wrap the gift. You just remember to bring me some cake and one of those single brothers roaming around at that reception."

I agreed, we gave each other a hug, and then I grabbed my coat, and was off again. I made it to the wedding within fifteen minutes, five minutes before it was scheduled to begin, found a seat on the bride's side of the room, and waited patiently for another hour before the wedding party arrived at the church.

BIANCA

The next week went by fast. Between partying, dating, attending class and working I barely remembered what day it was. But on Thursdays, like clockwork, Steve would call to remind me. He was my Friday night date. We were going to the Music Hall theatre to see Najee this weekend, so he couldn't wait to boast. "Yeah baby, are we still on for tomorrow night? You know I got these tickets to see Najee in concert and I know how much you like him. So I got us seats in the mezzanine where there will be a buffet dinner set out for his fans and he's signing autographs personally."

I had completely forgot about the concert. I was too busy to even get excited with this reminder call. Sometimes Steve could just take the fun out of everything with the way he bragged about things too. I knew he was campaigning for my sex. I'd given it some thought a few times, but he was so transparent and boring I couldn't help but believe his sex would be the same.

Putting on my fake impressed demeanor, I giggled and responded," Yeah baby I remember and I've got something real special to wear just for you. What time will you be picking me up?"

"I'll get there at seven."

Keeping up the charade, I rolled my eyes and responded with a grin, "Make it six thirty. It's been a whole week since I've seen you."

After the concert, we walked hand and hand to his car in the parking lot across the street from the theater. It was a beautiful black, four door, Diamante. It had leather seats and a sweet sound system. I loved how the bells would chime when he would open the car door for me and I'd slide into the sweet scent of cherries. It was cold that night and late. Steve had a few glasses of wine, but not nearly enough for me to feel uncomfortable with him driving home. As we cruised up Gratiot Avenue, Steve reached over to caress my inner thigh. I was wearing a short, black, fitted dress that I had borrowed from Sarah. He believed that I would have sex with him before the night was over because of the lap dance and show I had put on prior to the concert. After the four glasses of white Zinfandel that I had consumed and hearing Najee, I was beginning to change my mind about Steve. I had told Chauncey that I was going out with my cousins who were here from out of town, so he was not expecting me to be home early. Why not give Steve some? It had been almost six months. He had spent more money on me than Chauncey ever had and I gave myself to him on a regular basis.

In the midst of my sexual thoughts a car spun out from nowhere and ran into the back of us. Steve lost control of the car and jumped the curb near an abandoned building. I was screaming and holding on to my head when we spun in circles and hit the fire hydrant on the corner. I was shaken up a bit, but Steve acted as though nothing had happen. He looked over at me and asked if I was O.K., then got out to check on the car that so carelessly hit us. The two teenagers that were in the two-door sports car were bleeding and screaming as though he'd hit them. The police showed up twenty minutes later and we made a police report. One of the teenagers had stolen his mom's new car and they had been drinking a lot and joy riding. The whole accident caused so much commotion that the whole neighborhood came out to see what was going on. After the police finished their questioning and the EMT checked everyone out, Steve and I were free to leave. The teenagers, however, needed to be taken away in the ambulance.

I was so shaken up by everything that had transpired, I told Steve to take me home right away and I never called him again. Whenever he would call me, I would have Sarah tell him I was not home. I started to ask myself questions like, "What would you have told Chauncey if you ended up in the hospital?" "How would he take it if he knew you were out with another man?" It was then I knew that I cared more for Chauncey than I had originally thought. He had cheated on me in high school and I had carried that grudge for six years. What the hell was I doing? What was I thinking?

When I saw him again I began to appreciate him for everything I thought he was to me. I stopped dating other men. I called him every day. I made plans to see him every day. I played with his spoiled and rotten daughter. I pretended to like his mom, who had made it clear how much she disliked me. I cooked for him and her and cleaned their house. I would even give him money and let him drive my car for days at a time. Things were moving so fast. When people would caution, "slow down," I would move faster. It had not dawned on me how stupid I had become until he began to make plans for us which, included my dropping out of school, and getting a full time job. I had just started the second semester of my last year. I would have my bachelor's degree at the end of the next semester, I was not about to let him mess that up for me.

I took my dilemma to my roommate, Sarah, because I knew she would set me straight. But when I started to tell her about him and his plans, I had to stop *myself* and say, "What the hell is wrong with you?" Sure Chauncey and I had dated since high school, and yeah he has been around for six years, but what accomplishments has he made in those six years? Well let's see, he has a six year old daughter as a result of a one night stand in high school. He dropped out of college, moved back home with his parents, quit his job to avoid paying child support, and has never registered to vote nor obtain a legal driver's license.

After five minutes of ranting and raving on what a loser, with a capital "L", Chauncey was, Sarah began to cough and cry from laughing. "Bianca!" She said, "Leave dat dude alone!"

I took her advice. I dumped him and didn't look back. Two weeks later, I went to the bathroom and discovered a green and foul smelling discharge in my panties. "What the fuck?" I immediately called the doctor and got an appointment for later that afternoon.

BIANCA

WHAT GOES AROUND COMES BACK AROUND!

"Chlamydia! Can this shit be cured? What will happen? What is going on? Oh! God help me," were all the things I could think of to say to the doctor as she examined my vagina.

"Yes, Bianca, it looks like chlamydia to me, but I won't know for sure until we get the culture sample back from the lab and that may take up to ten days."

"Let me get this straight, you just told me that you believe I have some shit, but you don't know for sure, and you can't do anything for me for another week? Are you crazy? What am I suppose to do about this discharge and foul ass smell?"

"Well this is the chance you take when you have unprotected sex. I understand how you may feel, but this is all I can tell you right now. I will write you a prescription for an antibiotic; take it twice a day for ten days. When I get your results back I will call you but you may need to come back in if it is something else. Your urine sample indicates that you are not pregnant but you need to consider using condoms if you are going to be having sex. The pills don't protect you from STDs."

Dr. Anderson was right. She knew me better than I'd known myself. It was almost like she was a second mother to me. She had been my doctor since the day I turned sixteen years old. That was also the day my mom came home from work early and caught me with a boy in the house. She was furious. Besides death, my only other option was to begin taking birth control pills.

Dr. Anderson was also there six months later, when a car, ran a red light, had hit me. She and my mom eventually became really good friends. She treated my injuries and offered my mom plenty of support and encouragement.

When we settled out of court, I was awarded 100,000 dollars. After paying my attorneys, I was left with a little over 60,000 dollars. My parents placed the money into a CD at the bank until I was eighteen years old. That's how I learned to budget money and pay my own way through college. I was no fool. My parents were divorced and I knew my mom couldn't afford to send me to school. So everything Chauncey was talking about when he advised me to quit school went all over my head.

It was my fault for trusting his punk ass. But how was I to know that while I was cheating on him, he was out cheating on me. Why didn't he use a condom with whomever he was cheating on me with? I always made it a point to use one when I cheated on him.

I called Chauncey the moment I unlocked my car door. "Hello! Chauncey, you bastard! I'm leaving the doctor's office and she told me that I have a STD. You and I need to talk today!"

"Hah! Hah! I fooled you. I'm not in at the moment but if you leave a message I will get back with you as soon as possible, PEACE!" BEEP.

"Unfuckingbelieveable, the one time I desperately need to talk to your silly ass, you're not home. This is B. give me a call. It's important. Bye."

I drove home in tears. How could this be happening to me? I had not given myself up to anyone besides Chauncey in months. Who else could he be sleeping with? Who would want him? Then it clicked - his scanky baby's momma, that's who! Oh shit, not that bitch again.

After the prom she and I never got along. When she had Cicily, his daughter, she refused to let Chauncey see her unless he promised to break up with me. "I want us to be like a family," she would say.

When he refused her proposal, she threatened to move to Mississippi to live with her grandmother and take the baby with her. I said, "Great!"

But Chauncey wanted to be a father to his child. Eventually, she backed off, but I have caught her trying to test our relationship a few times since then. She would page him just to put in "hello." She would call him to come over to change light bulbs that were "too high to reach." She would even call him when Cicily was sick and ask him to spend the night with them so their daughter could have both of her parents there with her. It was ridiculous. I hated him and her for that shit!

When I got home the phone was ringing as I turned the key in the lock.

"Hello."

"Bianca, baby what's wrong? You said it was an emergency. What's up?"

For a moment I was flattered by the concern in his voice, but he didn't care about me enough to at least use a condom when he was out fucking around on me.

"Chauncey I went to the doctor's office today and she thinks I have a sexually transmitted disease."

"What?"

"She says I have chlamydia. Chauncey, you're the only person I've been with, so you tell me what?"

"Bianca, can we do this in person? I really would like to sit down and discuss this rationally."

"What do we have to discuss Chauncey? Have you been sleeping around or not? No, don't answer that. I know you have or I wouldn't be having this problem, would I?"

"I love you girl! Can I come over, so we can talk?"

That is when I broke down. I couldn't help myself. Tears flooded my face like a raging river. I couldn't talk and I was weak and limp. Sarah took the receiver from me and hung up the phone. She made me some green tea and I climbed into bed.

Two days had gone by before I opened my bedroom door again. The apartment was quiet. Sarah was gone and the only sound in the house was the humming of the refrigerator in the kitchen. I ran myself a hot bath and surrounded myself with lit candles. I put on the radio on 98.7 and listened to the jazz music as its soothing melodies filled the house. I ran the water through my fingers gently and hummed to the sweet sound of Fourplay's "Making Love Between the Sheets" with Chaka Kahn. "You have got to pull yourself together girl!" I said aloud to myself.

BIANCA

Before I knew it December had come and gone. Sarah had taken the tree and decorations down. The eggnog was gone, and the family gathering was a blur. It was January. I didn't even recall watching the ball drop. Since I was home alone I ordered a pizza and began to read *Acts of Faith*, by Iyanla Vanzant. It was a Christmas gift from my aunt and this was the first time I had taken the time to read it. As I flipped through the pages, I was suddenly taken by one of the affirmations. It said something like "you are a survivor, you were the only one that made it out of all the other 20,000 sperm." I thought to myself, "Wow! That was deep." As I continued to read, I found many others that I thought were speaking directly to me it was at that moment I began to reflect on everything that had happened to me and decided it was time for a change. It was a new year and time for me to clean house. I wrote down those affirmations and placed them on my bedroom mirror so that every morning that I looked in it, I could reassure myself that everything would be O.K.

When Valentine's Day rolled around, I was determined not to be depressed any longer. I was convinced that going out with Sarah and the girls, and remembering my affirmations would be all that I needed. Besides, it wasn't like I had anything or anyone else to occupy my time that day. At least with the girls, I could go club hopping, get some drinks, male bash, and talk about old times. I was tired of being down. I was tired of being home alone. Hell, I was tired of going out with the same old men. However, once we arrived at the club, I wished I had called one of them to take me out. There were couples everywhere, holding hands and rubbing noses. There were couples that looked like it was their first date. There were no single men in sight. "Who in the hell decided to make up this holiday anyway?" I asked. I was lonelier then, than any other time that year.

By the beginning of March I had started a new job with Ford Motor Company. It was an intern position at the Dearborn office complex. I worked five days and attended classes two nights every week. I enjoyed working with the other accountants. They were an encouragement for me. I also began attending church every Sunday with my grandmother. I was picking out and dating new flavors of the month on Fridays and Saturdays. But I decided that I wouldn't put my feelings into any one of them. I also decided not to ever use the word "love" again unless I really felt I meant it.

When Tonya suggested letting my hair grow, I agreed and let her highlight it with blond to accent my hazel nut color eyes. I joined a gym and worked out four nights a week. I was definitely determined to turn my life around. However, the thought of Chauncey's betrayal would often take over and I would be left depressed all over again.

I would often come home at night and pick up the phone to call him then hang up. After following this routine over and over, Sarah advised me to simply dial the number so that I could put an end to this madness.

"Hello."

"Hi, Chauncey. It's me Bianca. I think it's time for us to talk."

"Oh yeah? You finally decided to work things out between us?"

Right then I knew it was a mistake for calling his sorry ass, and I regretted taking Sarah's advice.

"No, I need us to talk so that I can move on with my life."

"What do you mean?"

"I need closure on this Chaucey. I've been sitting around distraught about all this mess. I don't even know what happened between us. One minute we thought we were in love and the next minute I was being told that I had a STD. What happened? How could you have done that to me?"

"What do you mean how would I do that to you. Please don't pretend that you were faithful to me. I just gave you a taste of your own medicine. Yeah I should have used a condom and that was stupid on my part, but you have been screwing around on me for years."

"Chauncey, what are you talking about?" As though I didn't have a clue.

"I'm talking about the men you've been dating and spending the night with. That's what! You thought you were being a player when in actuality you were the one being played."

"No, Chauncey I don't think I'm a player. I think that I'm a woman who needs an explanation. Why do you think that I cheated on you?"

Tracey, the "big old pimp," also taught me to never admit to anything when you've been caught until your accuser has showed you solid proof.

"Are you saying that you've never crept out on me?"

"Yes, that is exactly what I'm saying."

"O.K. B. Let me come over and show you that you are a liar!"

"No, that won't be necessary. I know that I have never cheated on you Chauncey. I would never want to cause you any pain like that." I thought that sounded good. He would fall for that for sure.

"Well then you come over here. If you're not lying, you'll let me show you why I did what I did and then you can tell me why you did what you did. We can make up and make love."

"You must be crazy. You will never, ever, get another chance to taste my shit again!"

"Are you coming?"

"Yeah! I'll come over Chauncey, but know that after we clear the air my clothes will still be on."

I hung up the phone and told Sarah where I was going to be. She and I always made it a point to inform each other of our whereabouts. With all of the things you see on the news about ex-boyfriends killing their girlfriends I didn't want to take any chances. I didn't know what frame of mind he was in nor what kind of evidence he may have had on me. Sarah told me to take her pocketknife.

BIANCA

When I pulled up in the driveway, Chauncey came out of the side door and walked to the passenger side of my car. He was wearing a black shearling coat with a matching cap, jeans, and a pair of tall black leather Timberland boots. I unlocked the doors and let him in.

"Hey! It took you long enough!"

"O.K. I'm here now, what kind of proof do you believe you have on me?"

"Let's go for a ride. I'll show you."

"Look I don't have time for these games. I just wanted us to clear the air so that I don't have to walk around wondering who in the hell you slept with. Why you didn't protect yourself? Didn't you care enough about me not to put my shit in jeopardy?"

"B. Why do you keep pretending that you are an angel? You don't even know for sure if I'm the one that gave you the shit or not. I know you've been cheating on me. I saw you leaving the guy's house a few times. To prove it to you I'll show you where he lives."

"Who? You haven't seen me leaving anyone's house."

Thinking "Oh! Shit" to myself.

"Oh I haven't? You don't know a guy named Will that lives off of Michigan Avenue?"

My mouth fell open. How could he know about William? Did he really see me leave his house? I had forgot about Will. He was the guy I met at the mall back in September. He was in the Footlocker shoe store when Sarah and I were looking for gym shoes for her nephew. He wasn't all that cute in the face, but he had wads of money in his pockets. Sarah called them "gangster rolls." He was a big guy. He had to have weighed close to three hundred pounds. He was dressed in baggy black Guess jeans with a matching Guess sweatshirt and some real nice black Kenneth Cole casual boots. His leather jacket said Pelle Pelle on the back and he smelled like the sweet scent of Eternity for Men.

He stood in line in front of us with two of his friends. One of them turned around to talk to Sarah and noticed me standing next to her. "Damn! Will did you see these fine young ladies come in here?" As he threw the cashier two hundred dollar bills, he glanced over his shoulder. "Naw man, I didn't see 'em." He stuck out his hand to collect his change, but turned to face me and said, "The one in the red shirt is mine; she's cute. I'd give her the world! Baby! What's your name?"

"Bianca. Bianca Havin. But, you can call me Miss B. Havin, if you nasty."

We smiled at each other, then he said, "Miss B. Havin, huh? I'm Will, but you can call me daddy from now on!"

So I did! Whenever things didn't quite go the way I had planned, and money was tight, I'd call "daddy". He told me he was in real estate. He bought houses, fixed them up and rented them out or sold them. He was always very generous with his money and never really wanted anything in return. He was nine years older than me, so he only asked me to go out with him a few times just to show his friends that he could date a fine young woman. He kept his distance, I guess to avoid falling in love with a "Tender Roni," like myself. So, I knew that Chauncey may have seen me leave his house, but his ass was still the prime suspect in the sexually transmitted disease case.

"Fuck you Chauncey! Yeah, you may have seen me leave his house, but he and I are only friends. We have never had sex and you can ask him that yourself! You're the only one that has cheated in this relationship, twice! Once, with that bitch Kelly and this time with only God knows who!"

"Are you still talking about that shit? Bianca that was six fucking years ago! Please let that shit go already! I can't do anything about that anymore. I've apologized over and over again. If that guy was just your friend why were you kissing his big ass on the front lawn?"

"Chauncey, he has been there for me when I really needed him. I have never had to fuck to get him to do anything for me. If you saw me kissing him then it was only on the side of his face and nothing more. The question at hand is, who did you sleep with and why?"

"O.K., B. If you really want to know who it was, I'll tell you."

"Thank you, that's all I want to know and then we are through for good!"

"I wouldn't say all of that! You and I have too much history for us to end on something as simple as this shit! I've cheated on you before and we've gotten through it. Why would you want to end us now? If you love me, then stay with me. Be a woman and just accept me as I am. I made a mistake, but I thought you were cheating on me! What was I suppose to do?"

"You were to come and talk to me! Ask me what the hell was going on? Where were you at to see me anyway?"

"I was leaving my boy's house. He lives four houses down, and across the street from your so-called friend! He was cutting my hair and his girl and her friend from school stopped by. They were down here visiting from Eastern Michigan University. When I saw you leaving ol' dude's house, I was hurt. I went back in and started hollering at his girl's friend. She was a freak. I should have known not to fuck with her ass. Her and her girl started taking their clothes off and dancing on his tables and shit! She even took one of our beer bottles and put it in her vagina! I was confused and turned on, so I fucked! Yeah it was stupid, but I was trippin' baby, I'm sorry. I'm sorry!" Chauncey had tears in his eyes. I had never seen him cry before, so I was moved by it. He leaned over, we held each other and cried.

BIANCA

"You are a complete sucker for this guy, Bianca. What's wrong with you?"

"I don't know Sarah. I guess I really do love him. He was sincere. He was hurt. It's not like I haven't been cheating on him, too. We both were just trippin'. Things are going to be different now. We talked for hours last night and held each other for what seemed like the first time. It's cool now. We are going to work things out. That's going to be the man I marry. You watch and see."

"No, Bianca the only thing that I believe I will see is you crying and depressed again. This guy is bad news. I can feel it. You need to just leave him alone. I thought you were "cleaning house" and starting your new year with new men. Why are you going back to him?"

"I don't know. It's just something about him that I can't resist." I knew Sarah was right. I didn't need to be with Chauncey any longer. My own parents have told me that a thousand times. Neither one of them liked him. Usually if my mom doesn't like something, my dad will, and vice versa. That should have been my clue a long time ago. I went into my bedroom to sulk. I picked up my book of affirmations and began to flip through the pages.

If you continue to drink from a dirty cup you will get sick.

That statement, like all the others, gave me more insight into my situation with Chauncey. I wasn't happy with him, yet I continued to drink from his cup and get sick. I dated other men but always held on to him. What is it about this man that I can't get enough of? Was I afraid to be alone?

I lay in bed and began to pray. I asked God to tell me what to do? I asked him to guide me, and remove all obstacles in the way of me doing what He has intended for me to do. I asked him to show me how to love myself. I asked him to show me how to love others. I asked God to remove all negativity from my life. I simply asked for God's help in everything I did or thought I wanted to do. I thanked him for my parents, family, friends, clothes, car, apartment, health, education, and wealth. That night I spoke to God until I could no longer find the words to say. Then I cried myself to sleep.

The next day, Sarah and I decided to go to the mall. "Shopping will make you feel better," she said. I agreed. "There's a psychic fair at Eastland Mall. Maybe they can see our futures," she teased.

As we entered the corridors of the mall, two tables were lined up side by side with small lines of people who were anxious to hear what life had in store for them. One of the fortunetellers had a crystal ball, while the other read palms and tarot cards. Sarah and I decided to check out the woman with the cards.

"Hello ladies, which one of you wants to go first?"

"Me," I chimed. "How much for the tarot card readings?"

"O.K. Tarot card readings are $20."

"Are you any good?"

"Yes, my predictions are 90% accurate."

"Tell me something about myself, and then I'll decide if you're worthy of my $20."

Reluctantly, she said, "You just broke up with your boyfriend. He was a dog. He deserves everything that will come to him."

Sarah and I both looked at each other and said, "Wow, how did you know that?"

"He cheated on you, but it's O.K. He'll get what he deserves real soon. The woman he's with now is going to use him and kick his butt!"

"What! He's seeing someone else already? O.K. lady, here's my money. Tell me more about his punk ass."

"No! I need you to just let him go! He's no good for you any more. Think of three questions that you'd really like to know the answers to. Then, I'd like you to tell me two of them and keep the last one to yourself."

Sarah looked at me with an "I told you so eye." I ignored her. I began to think of 100 things I'd like to know the answers to. How could I possibly narrow my curiosity down to three questions?

A few minutes went by before Madam Mallory gave me her deck of cards and asked me to shuffle them. When I was done I passed them to her and she asked me to cut them in half. As I handed her the stack of cards I told her what I wanted to know.

"I want to know who I will marry and where will I work?" She smiled at me. Then spread the deck of cards out in front of her and said, "The man you will marry already knows you and is waiting patiently for his chance to pursue you."

"He already knows me? Is it someone that I have dated in the past?"

"No, but he is someone that has dated women like you in the past. So, he knows what kind of woman you are, but will accept you anyway! Let him tame you. He is the only one that will be able to give you the love that you are looking for."

BIANCA

Madame Mallory told me things that were unbelievable. I was very pleased with her responses to my questions. When we got ready to leave she gave us several scriptures to read from the bible and assured us that we would both have fruitful and prosperous lives.

By May, I followed her advice and had finally gotten myself together. I let go of Chauncey in March. I graduated and took my CPA exam. I passed with flying colors, and turned twenty-one. I had also accepted a full time position at Ford Motor Company with a starting salary of $40,000.

To celebrate my accomplishments, Sarah and I decided to go out for drinks at a new sports bar that had opened up in Southfield. We went to their Friday night Happy Hour to be among the after work crowd. Since I'd blown up, we no longer felt the need to hang out with the college crowds that packed places later in the evenings.

I wore my navy blue A-line silk skirt. It slightly

hugged my hips and swayed from left to right with each step. My white silk blouse complimented my hourglass figure, and my new navy pumps added another 2” to my firm long legs. I had more confidence in myself that day, than I’d ever had.

We sat at a small table next to the bar and ordered two glasses of white Zinfandel. The place was packed with men and women of all ages, race, and class. While the older gentlemen wore suits and ties, some of the younger guys had the freedom of wearing casual shirts and slacks. Sarah and I were getting attention from both age groups. When the waitress brought our drinks over, she informed us that our bill had been paid. Two older gentlemen, who were sitting at the bar, picked up the tab. I smiled and mouthed the words “thank you” to both of them, but showed no further interest. Sarah, on the other hand, found the one in the black suit appealing and went to thank him up close and personal. She approached him with a sexy walk. I said, "Later girl. Go do your thang!”

I took a sip of my wine and casually bobbed my head to the slow music coming from the speakers of the jukebox near the pool tables. I started to sing along with Anita Baker when the waitress approached my table again.

“You’re getting all the attention tonight girl!”

“What do you mean?”

“Well, this is another drink for you and the gentleman over there with the dreads says to tell you, hello.”

"Where?"

"By the window."

I slowly turned to follow her pointing finger and thought my eyes were playing tricks on me. My heart must have skipped four beats.

"I know he's not pretending to be shy. He is all that and a bag of chips. Why did he send you over here?" I questioned the waitress.

"I don't know, but he's been watching you since you sat down."

"Tell him I said thanks for the drink, but I don't like shy men. If he's interested, he needs to come over here and say so."

"O.K., but I know you're not going to let him get a way, are you?"

"I will if he doesn't come over here."

The waitress gave me a "you go girl" look and went to relay my message to the brother.

To tell the truth I didn't know what I was thinking. He was gorgeous! If I had seen him first I would have attacked him. I love a man in dread locks. I've never dated one, but there is a certain mystery and intrigue in a guy who is brave enough to do that to his hair. He has to have balls bigger than the moon, and a penis that's proportionate to them. I got moist just thinking about the positions I wanted to be in with him. I turned around in my chair so that I could put his face into the freaky mental picture I was having when I noticed that he was already on his way to my table.

The song on the jukebox appropriately

switched to R. Kelly's extended remix version of "You're Body is Calling," as he slowly approached me. He was six feet three inches tall and slightly bow legged, with a walk that would make Denzel Washington look clumsy. I stood up only to meet him half way, but when I stopped, I was so close to him I could have easily slipped my tongue in his mouth. He was a nice dark chocolate, with dark brown eyes that said, "B., I want to make love to you all night long." I stuck my hand out to introduce myself and to get a better look at his big broad shoulders and arms. The only thing that was going through my mind was, "How in the hell could I be so lucky today?"

"Hello, my name is Kyle Sinclair. How are you?"

"I'm fine, Kyle. How are you?"

"Well, to tell the truth, I'm a little nervous, but I'm O.K. What's your name?"

With a devilish grin, "I'm Bianca. Bianca Havin. But my friends like to call me Miss B. Havin. Are you alone?"

"No, I'm here with some of my buddies, but when I saw you come in I wanted to be here with you."

"He's not all that shy," I thought.

"Oh! O.K., well, let's sit down and talk. Thanks for my drink. What are you having? The next round is on me." "Ginger ale."

"Are you serious? Ginger ale and what?"

"Just ginger ale. I don't drink."

"Oh! I'm sorry. Do you have a problem with

alcohol?"

"No, I just don't drink it."

"How can you come into a bar and not have a drink?"

"I came here to eat and hang out with my friends. I was baptized and saved eight months ago and decided never to subject myself to alcohol again."

"Sorry. Is it a touchy subject for you?"

"No, not at all. But, I didn't come over here to discuss that. I'd like to talk about you."

"What would you like to know?"

"Everything!"

"Everything like what?"

"Do you play pool?"

"Yes, would you like to play?"

"Yeah, let's check out the competition over there? Maybe we can run the tables."

"O.K. I'm wit dat!"

As we strolled to the rear of the bar, Kyle gently placed his palm on the small of my back. We both ignored the jealous stares of men and women as we passed through to crowd lined up to place their orders at the bar.

"Are you old enough to be in here?"

"What do you mean? They would not have let me in, if I were not old enough to get in! Are you trying to ask me how old I am?"

"No, a gentleman would never ask a woman her age."

"I'm twenty one."

"Why were you sitting alone?"

"I'm not alone. My roommate is here. We're celebrating life and good fortune!"

"Oh!" He replied, as he selected two sticks from the wall. "That sounds nice. What exactly is the good news?"

"I accepted a new job offer."

"Where?"

"Ford. I'm an accountant."

"Wow! You're twenty-one, beautiful, and smart. Are you single?"

"Yes, I am. Why did you try to pretend you were shy Mr. Sinclair? I think you've said exactly what you've meant to say since you've approached me."

"I never said I was shy. I said I was nervous."

"Why?"

"Because you are so sexy, and pretty, I assumed that you'd be difficult to talk to."

"You think pretty women are hard to talk to?"

"No. I thought you would be difficult to talk to because all of the men in here have been sweating you. I guess I didn't know how you would respond to me sweating you too!"

As he leaned down to break the balls, I thought, "You'd be surprised at how well I'd respond to you sweating on me."

After an hour of interesting conversation and laughs, it seemed as though Kyle and I were the only two people in the room. We had both blocked out the other 200 people in the bar. I was glad he came to talk to me. I enjoyed the game and his company.

"I'd like for us to be friends."

"I'd like that too." He smiled, and two gorgeous deep dimples appeared in his smooth and even toned skin. "I'd like to have you all to myself."

Just when I was about to tell him the X-rated version of what I wanted, Sarah approached us.

"Hey girl! Are you about ready to go?"

"Yeah, I'm ready when you are. Meet my new friend, Kyle."

"Oh! Hello, Kyle." Flirting, "How are you?"

"Uh, fine. O.K. B., since your friend is back I'll leave
you two alone."

"That's Miss B. Havin, for you. Do you want to exchange phone numbers?"

"Yeah! I do. I was hoping you'd say that! Do you think we can hook up tonight?"

Here's my card, my home number is on the back. I'll be there at 8:00 and I'll be waiting anxiously for your call."

"O.K. Kyle, I'll call you at 8:01."

Sarah and I both watched Kyle ease away from the pool table before we gave each other that, "I'd love to fuck him!" look.

"Damn girl! All the action was over here. I wasted my time going to talk to that old guy at the bar. He was married with three kids."

"Yeah, well down Fido. You move, you lose. Mr. Kyle is all mine now!"

"I hear dat! So you want to go over to Fridays to get something to eat before we head home or what?"

"Yeah! That sounds good," I responded.

When I looked back to get one last glance at him I noticed he was watching me, too. We both waved and smiled to each other. Sarah and I began to giggle as we turned to exit the building.

"I'll go visit him later to get dessert!"

KYLE

"Wow man, who was that? She was hot!"

"Well man, I'm hoping that will be the mother of my children someday."

Steve and Roger both laughed. Then Roger spoke, "Yeah right man, she's too fast for all of that. She doesn't look like the settling down type to me. You'd better be careful. Don't get caught up in that one. She'll rip your choirboy ass to pieces and break your heart, just like all the others. I think you like to pick that type of woman."

"What do you mean?"

"Don't you remember how your last girl played you? You always pick the same freaked out ass type of woman. Man, you need to get yourself a nice girl who likes to go to church, like you."

"Oh, yeah."

"Yeah! She's a freak. Everybody was trying to push up on that. You wouldn't stand a chance with her."

"You think so, huh? I haven't always been a choirboy, son. Don't sleep on my skills. You know I used to be a player, too!"

"Yeah, O.K. You just be careful. You know you

haven't had any pussy in months now. Don't go proposing to her too soon. She looks wild!"

"You let me worry about dat. She may just need a little taming. That's all. She's the one though."

"The one for what?" Steve and Roger grimaced.

"The one I've been praying for. Miss Bianca is going to be my wife!"

"You'll change your mind about that one brother. No man wants a freak for a wife. What the hell is wrong with you?"

"Nothing is wrong with me fool. What's wrong with you? Every man wants his wife to be a freak!"

Steve and Roger were both starting to piss me off, so I left them at the bar at 7:00. Besides, I wanted to make sure I was home in time for my call.

She was beautiful! Yeah, she was a little rough around the edges, but that's nothing that I hadn't come across before. I had to admit that I had a thing for the "round the way" qualities in a woman. My previous girlfriend, Tamara, wore big gold loop earrings and at least three rings on each hand. She had ghetto printed all across her forehead and was as mean as a pit bull. She was mad all the time. I couldn't recall a time when she wasn't angry. We had been dating for two years too long, and I was miserable. My cat mysteriously disappeared when she moved in. My friends would rag on me about being too soft with her. My parents would tell me she was too snotty and unappreciative. Every twenty-eight days, which was the schedule of her normal menstrual cycle, she'd turn into psycho woman. Her head would spin and she'd curse me out for the five days of its duration. On the weekends, she'd stay out with her girlfriends until three a.m. Then, she'd smoke weed, drink, and complain to no end the next morning. On top of that, she never wanted to work, cook, clean, nor have sex when I wanted to. So, Bianca couldn't be any worse. If anything, I'd be at least a little closer to a step in the right direction. We had so much in common. We were single, successful, and looking for love. Both of our parents were divorced and neither one of us had siblings. It was also blatantly obvious that she'd be willing to have sex upon request. I just hope she can accept my celibacy.

"While I awaited the call, I decided to turn on the television and watch some music videos. I showered and changed into my black Nike sweat suit. Then, I laid across my couch, slowly drifted into a coma like sleep, and envisioned her in a short red nightshirt with a matching red thong and slippers. Her hair was pinned up and she wore small diamond studs in each ear. I longed to kiss her neck and bright red painted lips. As I moved toward her, I heard bells ringing. At first, I thought they were wedding bells, but by the third chime, I realized it was my telephone. I jumped up to catch it before my answering service picked up the call.

BIANCA

I waited until 8:05 p.m. to dial up Mr. Sinclair just to make him wait a little longer. He answered on the third ring.

"Hello."

"Hi, Kyle? Were you sleeping?"

"Yes. I was taking a cat nap and dreaming about you."

"Yeah, right! That's the oldest line in the book." I laughed.

"That wasn't a line, I really was thinking of you."

"Do you even know who this is?"

"Of course I do! This is the future Mrs. Sinclair. Bianca Sinclair."

There was a pause.

"Wrong! This is Bianca Havin."

"O.K. I see you want to play hard to get! It's cool. I'm up for a challenge. What's up?"

"Oh, nothing. Sarah and I just got in so I called you like I promised."

"I'm happy you did."

"Would you like some company?"

"Yes , are you coming to see me?"

"Where do you live?"

"In Troy, are you familiar with the area?"

"Not really. Will you give me directions?"

"Sure. Take I-75 out to the Big Beaver exit, I'm across from the Somerset Mall. I'll meet you out front so you won't get lost. Do you have a cell phone?"

"Yes."

"Good. Call me when you are on your way. I'll come out and meet you and you can follow me back to my house."

"O.K. I'll be there in about twenty minutes. I know exactly where the mall is."

"You're a woman, of course you do! Hey! Did you eat yet?"

"Hah Hah! Yes, we went to eat after we left the bar."

"Would you like dessert?"

In my sexy tone of voice, "That's exactly what I'd like," was my response.

I don't think he was exactly sure about what I was trying to say, so he replied, "O.K. Do you like strawberries?"

"Yes, they are my favorite!"

"Good, I'll see you shortly."

As usual, I wrote down his information so that Sarah would know my exact whereabouts. Kyle seemed like a nice guy, but nice guys can be maniacs too. I changed into my red leggings and sweater, and began to pack a "just in case" over night bag.

"Why are you taking that?" Sarah questioned.

"I don't know if I'll be home tonight."

"Are you really going to spend the night?"

"I'm not sure yet! He's talking about strawberries. He might work me over girl! I hope I'll be to tired to drive home afterwards, if you know what I mean!"

"Damn! I thought you said he was saved. Well you'll definitely have to tell me all about it tomorrow. Girl, he is too sexy!"

"We'll see! You know these brothas be out here claiming they into the church and then backslide behind closed doors. I just hope he's not one of those, cute in the face, sexy as hell men, who come quick."

We sighed, hugged, and gave each other a high five. "You remember the last guy you ran off to meet. Did he even last two minutes?"

"Who, Roy? Hell naw, he didn't last that long. He didn't even get a chance to penetrate. All he did was rub his little penis up against my legs. Ugh! Sarah, why did you even bring that shit up? I will be so upset if this turns out to be a repeat of that night."

As I walked to my car, I began to recall, in detail, the night I spent with Roy. He worked in the same building with me on the fifth floor. At first glance, he would appear attractive, smart, athletic, and sexy. However, when you got up close and personal, the way I did that night, you'd see the young and timid virgin in him. It was awful! He had no clue how to please a woman. I didn't even know there were men like that until I came across him.

He approached me one day on the elevator with some sorry line. He wanted to know what floor I worked on and what position I held with the company. When I told him I was an intern, he offered to buy me lunch. He basically bugged the hell out of me until I agreed to go out with him for dinner. If I had not been so down and desperate for dick at the time, I would have sent him on his way the moment he said, “hello.”

He took me to a restaurant in St. Clair Shores called Andiamo’s. We ordered a couple of steaks and a bottle of red wine. We weren’t into the meal five minutes before he leaned in close to me and whispered, “You want to go back to my place after this?”

I thought, “What the hell. How bad could it be? If anything, he could be my new Friday or Saturday. We’d eat and sleep together a few times and then I’d switch to a new guy in a few months.” So I responded, “Sure, do you live close by?”

What a disaster! He was thirty years old and still lived at home with his mom. We had to sneak into a musty and dark basement, where he slept on a twin size bed. He had posters of naked women plastered on the walls, and a crate of playboy books and porno movies sat in the corner. He turned on his clock radio and held me close. I could feel his hard as a rock, little penis swell in his pants.

“You smell so good, Bianca. I’d love to lick you

all over." He pulled me down on the bed next to him and awkwardly undressed me. He nibbled my ears and kissed my neck. Then, he slid my bra strap down my arm and began to lick my armpits.

"What are you doing?"

"Just relax baby. I'm going to make love to you like no man ever has."

He unzipped his pants and pulled "peewee" out of the front hole of his boxers.

"Oh! Baby you like that don't you? Can't nobody do you like I can baby. I'm going to rock your world!"

Two minutes later, his boxers were wet, and I was pissed and ready to go home.

I closed my eyes and began to say a silent prayer that Kyle would not be timid in bed like Roy. It had been a long time since I'd had a good sex partner. That whole thing with Chauncey and men like "Mr. Two Minute" made me hold on to my goods real tight. But I definitely wanted to loosen my grips with Kyle. I wanted him to touch me in places I'd forgotten about and make me holler until the neighbors complained. I wanted to be teased, licked, and kissed. Most of all, I wanted him to hold me in those strong arms so tight that I'd feel safe from all harm and yearn for more of his affection. I felt it was time for me to have that in my life. I didn't want to spend another holiday, weekend, day, night, hour, or minute alone.

I would often dream of the man who filled every void in my life. At night I'd pray for him and ask God to keep him safe. He was my inner peace and joy. Although we'd never met, I believed he was tall and strong. However, in my dreams, his face was never clear. We'd laugh, talk, and share secrets with each other. We'd make love in the grass on breezy spring days and in the rain on hot and sticky summer evenings. I felt overwhelmed with love and bliss. He was the man who made me never want to be with another. I didn't know if this man would be Kyle or not. However, I knew that whoever he was, we'd meet soon.

I let out a long sigh and reached down to turn on the radio. I searched through the stations until I found something soothing. When I heard Chante Moore's "I'm what you need," I felt it was appropriate for the ride. I turned the volume up and hummed all the way to my destination.

BIANCA

When I stepped out of the car, he assisted and closed the door to my red Ford Probe. He said I was gorgeous. He loved the way my beautiful brown hair moved as I walked.

"Do you think you would've got lost if I didn't meet you?"

"No, I shop at Somerset all the time. Your house is beautiful! Do you live alone?"

"Yes, I do. Please, come in. Let me show you the place. I believe you'll be spending a lot of time here from now on. So please make yourself comfortable."

"You're quite the character, Kyle. You're so sure of yourself. How do you know you'll want to invite me again? We only met a few hours ago."

"Let's just say, I'm a man who knows exactly what he wants and isn't afraid to work for it. So, you can let down your guard down B. "Resistance is futile." Don't you believe in love at first sight?"

Ignoring him, I pushed him aside and said, "Only in the movies and corny love novels. Wow! You have a Jacuzzi on your deck! You should've told me. I would've brought my swim suit."

"Well next time you can. Come on, let me

show you the rest. Then we can sit, talk, and eat our dessert."

"Dessert?"

"Yes, I made you and I a strawberry short cake for two."

"You really know how to put it on for a woman, Kyle."

After the tour of the house, we sat on the black leather sofa in the den, ate our dessert, and talked for hours. When I took my shoes off, he gently placed my feet in his lap and began to massage them.

"Oh! That feels so good! Can you do this everyday?"

"I'd be willing to do whatever you wanted me to, everyday."

"Oh! Now it comes out. I was beginning to think that you weren't attracted to me in that way."

"In what way?"

"You know, sexually."

"I'm sorry, Bianca. I didn't mean to give you the impression that I was referring to sex."

"So you don't want to have sex?"

"I'm not going to say that. What man wouldn't want you sexually? You're beautiful! Right now, I'm just interested in some of the other things you may have to offer as well. I like to take things slow. Sex is not my first priority."

"It isn't?"

"No. Unconditional love, honesty, respect, self control, spirituality, trust, and motivation are at the top of my list."

"That's different. Most guys would have been all over me by now. No one is interested in a commitment or a relationship nowadays. I've become so accustomed to the "date to mate" ritual that I've given up on loving and being loved by the opposite sex."

"Why? You are young, successful, smart, talented, and gorgeous. You could give Tyra Banks a run for her money any day. You deserve to be loved by a good man. Just as I deserve, a good woman."

"What's your definition of a good woman?"

"A good woman is someone who is nurturing, supportive, and self-motivated. She possesses all of the things at the top of my list and knows how to balance each one. She's innocent, yet full of intrigue. Someone I'd never get tired of. She's the one I'd live to love and would die without."

"Damn, Kyle. That was deep. Do you believe I'm that woman?"

"I believe that you possess all of those things. You just need the right person to bring it all out."

"Maybe you're right. It seems as though all I've been meeting lately are losers."

"Why? What happened in your last relationship? You said you were together for six years. He could not have been too much of a loser."

"Yes, he was. It just took me that long to see it, accept it, and let go."

"Well, they say everything happens for a reason. Maybe, you needed to let go of him so that you could grab a hold to me."

We laughed and he reached out to hold me. It was at that moment I realized that I didn't want him to ever let me go.

"So tell me about your ex. Why didn't she make the cut?"

"My ex was horrible and I don't want to ruin this beautiful night talking about an ugly situation."

"That bad, huh? O.K. Then let's talk about something else."

"O.K. What's your favorite movie?"

"Promise you won't laugh."

"I promise. Why? Is it one of those girly, crying flicks?"

"No, actually it's Menace to Society."

"No, really! Are you serious? Menace to Society is your favorite movie? Why?"

"It's true! I love Menace. I liked Jada's braids and her take-charge approach in the bedroom. That's something I would do. I also liked how tough Cain and O'dog were in the movie."

"Well, that's different. I thought you were going to say *Gone with the Wind* or something. You like the rough necks though, huh?"

"No, I like you and you're not rough and tough."

Frowning, "What do you mean? I'm the baddest mo' fo' around this town!"

"No, that would be the funny looking guy from *The Last Dragon*, Sho Nuff."

"Oh! I see you know your black movies."

"I know quite a few. So what's your favorite

movie?"

"Oh! You probably wouldn't know anything about my favorite movie. It's an old flick called, "Cabin in the Sky".

"No, I don't think I've seen that one. Do you have it here? What's it about?"

Grabbing the tape from the video cabinet, "Yeah, I do. In my opinion it's about appreciating the things you have and knowing what to do when God gives you second chances. Do you want to watch it?"

"Yeah, that sounds cool. Do you have any popcorn?"

"I think there's some in the kitchen. Please, feel free to grab whatever you want in there!"

"What about in here?" Looking at his private parts.

"Well I don't know if you should grab it, but I may let you touch it later. I don't usually put out on a first date."

"That's too bad. I was looking forward to seeing what I was working with."

He didn't respond verbally, but he did lick his lips at the thought of showing me exactly what I'd have to work with if I grabbed his penis.

"Down boy!" He mumbled to himself.

BIANCA

The next day Sarah tiptoed into my room, woke me up, and sat on the edge of the bed, "So girl, tell me what happened with you and Kyle. I went to bed last night before you came in. He must have turned you out!"

Rolling over to face her, "Sarah, you are so nasty! Actually we watched a movie and talked all night. I didn't get home until 7:30 this morning."

"Is that why you're just getting up at 2:00?"

"Yes, sorry I missed our Saturday morning work out. Kyle didn't want me to drive home late last night, so I slept there and drove home this morning."

"You talked all night? So what was up with the strawberries?" You didn't play any freaky games? That's not like you."

"Shut up! He made strawberry shortcake for dessert. He likes to cook. He's trying to open his own soul food restaurant in Troy. It was the first time a man has ever made anything for me. I thought it was cute!"

"That's cool. So, what did you talk about?"

"Everything! We stayed up until 4:00 a.m. He went to U of M for undergrad and grad school in their business program. He's twenty-nine years old. His father is a judge and his mother is a lawyer. He owns his own home and drives a beautiful white Lexus truck. He doesn't have any kids and is basically a pretty cool dude."

"Did you get to see him naked?"

"No, Kyle is a gentleman. I slept in the bed and he slept on the couch. He told me he didn't put out on a first date. That was also a first for me."

"I know. Do you think you'll be able to hang with this one? He almost seems to good to be true. Does he have any brothers?"

"No, sorry. He's an only child like me."

"Do you think he's the one?"

"To be honest with you Sarah, if I were ready to be in love again and settle down with one man, yes, Kyle would be the one. But, because that shit just hurts so much when they let you down, I'm not trying to feel that way for anyone. So for now, Kyle will only occupy my Friday nights. My heart is still on lock down."

Sarah and I talked and laughed about all the things that had transpired that night. Kyle was a very nice man, but at that time I meant what I said about falling in love again. I needed to learn to love myself.

I showered, put on a clean pair of pajamas, and changed the linen on my queen size bed. I went into the kitchen and made myself a BLT sandwich with a side of chips and poured a tall glass of Pepsi over ice. When I reached my bedroom, with food in hand, I climbed in bed and began to change the channels on my 32' color TV. My plan for the day was to simply relax, enjoy the peace and quiet and pamper myself. I thought about calling the mall to get an appointment with a masseuse. Unfortunately, my funds were too limited for that luxury. It would be wonderful if I knew a personal masseuse. That's when I recalled Kyle telling me he'd do whatever I wanted everyday while rubbing my feet last night. I shivered at the thought. His hands were so strong, yet gentle. He touched me with a passion I'd never felt before. I'd love to be held in his arms again. But, it would be to soon for me to call him. He would think I was desperate.

In the midst of my random, self-inflicted confusion, the phone rang. "Sarah, can you get that?" No response. "Sarah! Damn, where did she go? HELLO!"

"Hey baby! How are you? I've missed the sound of your voice. Where ya been? I've been trying to get in touch with you for a while now."

"Hey, to you too! Who is this?"

"It's Steve. Do you still remember me?"

"Oh! Hey Steve. Of course I remember you. What's up?"

"I was calling to see if you'd like to come out tonight. A friend of mine will be reading some of his poetry at Flood's. I'd like it very much if you'd accompany me. We can order some food, get a couple of drinks, and discuss what happened between us."

"What do you mean?"

"Well, you know! You just stopped calling me after the accident and you wouldn't accept my calls. I didn't know what was up. I figured you found a man or something. Are you seeing someone?"

"No, I'm not. But, if you thought I had a man, why'd you call?"

"I figured, it had been a few months now and maybe you'd broken up or something. You know relationships with you don't last that long."

What a turn off. What was he trying to say with that statement? Was I not worthy of a long lasting committed relationship? "Well what is that suppose to mean? You don't think I can keep a man?"

"No baby! I'm not saying that. Well, you know what, maybe I am saying that! I was damn good to you and you didn't want to keep me around. Shit! I figure if I was that good to you and you let me go, no other man was going to have a chance. We dated for about six months and I didn't even get a chance to smell, taste, or feel the pussy. I didn't think any other man would put up with that shit for longer than 2-4 months. So yeah! I guess that's why I figured you weren't still involved with anyone and I was right! So what's up? You want to go out tonight?"

"Hell naw, you bastard! How in the fuck can you call and insult me, then expect me to go out with you? This is why I stopped calling your arrogant ass. Please don't dial my phone number anymore, you pencil dick loser."

I hung up the phone and began to cry, not because I was sad, but because I was angry. Who in the fuck did he think I was? Did he think I would be O.K. with him telling me I couldn't keep a man? That bitch! I should call his punk ass back and tell him how much of a bitch he is for dating me that long without getting any of my good loving. Why do people call you with shit like that on days you just want a little peace? He had totallyruined my joy with that bullshit.

Ring. Ring. "WHAT?"

"Um, hi, Bianca?" Are you O.K.? This is Kyle."

"Oh! I'm sorry. Hello. No, Kyle I'm not O.K."

"Is there anything I can do?"

"Um, no not really? I'll be awright. I just need a little R & R. Rest and relaxation?"

"Exactly! I have an idea! Why don't you pack up some clothes and come over here."

"Are you serious? You just met me. I don't want to intrude on you. It's cool. I'm O.K."

"No, you're not! Come on over. It's not a bother. I'll buy you a bottle white Zinfandel, light some candles and give you a full body massage. We can even sit out in the Jacuzzi and talk about whatever or whoever has got you so worked up."

"I'd rather not!"

"Come over or talk?"

"Talk. I'd love to do the other things. What are you going to drink when I'm drinking wine?"

"I don't know. I don't care. Tonight is all about you. My wants will be met when you're pleased."

Damn, that sounded good. My joy had

instantly returned. I couldn't hang up the phone quick enough.

"I'm on my way!"

BIANCA

I left Sarah a note and packed in a hurry. The phone rang three more times before I left, but I refused to answer it. I was too stressed out and worked up to hear anyone else's petty bullshit. Going to Kyle's was exactly what I needed. I wanted to be with an interesting man in a pleasant atmosphere.

When I arrived, he came out to greet me and to carry my bags. He wore a white T- shirt and a pair of loose fitting dark blue jeans. His hair was pulled back, and his beard and mustache were both very neatly trimmed. He had what looked like a brand on his arm and the words OMEGA PSI PHI tattooed beneath it. It brought back memories of my college days. My girls and I would go over to the Que house on Ferry Street the first Friday of each month. Those men were so wild! I learned plenty of tricks and positions from a few of them. I knew, then, that Kyle would be no joke in bed. I looked up to God and whispered, "Thank you for answering my prayers!"

When we got inside, he put my bags down and put my coat in the closet. Then he turned to me, gently placed his hands around my waist, and pulled me close. "I'm glad you decided to come over. I've been thinking about you since you left this morning." Then, he leaned down and kissed my forehead and the tip of my nose. Before he could loosen his grip, I placed my hands on each side of his face and kissed him softly on the lips.

"I've been thinking about you, too."

"Don't tease me! You were probably telling your roommate that you were never going to call me again."

"No, I told her that I couldn't wait to see you again."

"Sure you did."

We kissed each other and smiled. Then he took my hand and led me to his bedroom where candles circled his king sized bed. He put on a jazz CD that was unfamiliar to me. "You can get undressed in here while I get your glass of wine. Would you like anything else?"

"Yes I would, but I'm trying to be a lady!"

"Bad girl! I'll be right back; just relax."

I took off my clothes and climbed in bed. I laid on top of his plush down comforter and smelled the sweet scent of his cologne on each pillow. When he returned, he had a glass of wine, a towel, and a bottle of jasmine scented oil. He got down on his knees and laid the towel on the floor. When I stood up and approached him to take my position he said, "You are definitely tryin' to tempt me aren't you? You look good enough to eat!"

"Now you're the one who's teasing."

"Please forgive me."

I took a sip of wine and laid on the towel. He put some oil in his hands and rubbed them together. I was anxious to feel his touch. Aroused, I let out a moan when I felt his warm, smooth palms caressing my bare skin.

"I won't be able to do this for long if you continue to make those sounds."

"Sorry. I'll behave."

Kyle was an honorable and respectful man. For an entire hour, he worked in silence and only placed his hands on my back, thighs, and feet. It was then that I knew I wanted to feel him inside of my warm and moist pleasure spot.

When he was finished, I drank the remainder of my wine and requested another. He left the room and returned with my drink and a plate of fruit. He grabbed my hand and we moved into the bathroom where a tub full of bubbles and rose petals awaited my arrival. I removed the towel and carefully climbed in the steaming hot water.

"Are you going to bathe me?"

"No," pointing to the plate of strawberries, "I'm going to feed you."

"That's too bad. I was looking forward to feeling your hands roam through my valley."

"I know."

As we playfully flirted back and forth for the duration of my bath, Kyle and I both knew that this was the start of something beautiful. At the end of the night, I was drunk, full, and horny. I threatened to put my clothes on and drive home if he did not sleep with me. So, as he slipped my nightgown over my head, he whispered softly in my ear, "O.K. Sweetheart, I will sleep with you." Unfortunately, all he did that night was sleep.

KYLE

Waking up next to Bianca was wonderful! I had to have lain in bed that morning and admired every curve of her body for at least an hour. Her skin glowed and her beautiful long brown hair delicately lay across my plush down feather pillows. She looked so peaceful and angelic. However, deep down I knew she was just the opposite. She had shared unbelievable stories with me. I had heard all about her ex-boyfriend Chauncey, and her weekend specials, Tom, Dick, and Harry. I knew she'd had her share of men. I also knew she had a hard time with trusting them. She wouldn't let herself fall in love again. But I wanted her. I wanted her more than I had ever wanted anything in life. So, if I rushed into things, I knew I would scare her away. She was protecting herself with a tough girl act. That's why I decided to take my time.

I got up at 9:30 and went into the bathroom to shower. Thinking about Bianca still lying in my bed with her nightgown on made me so horny I grabbed hold of my penis and silently took my time with it. My five-finger specials were becoming my best friends lately. I dried off, ironed my clothes, and met my boy Chuck at his barbershop around the corner about thirty minutes later. I wanted to get my hair cut before Bianca woke up."

"Oh! Today is the day, huh?"

"Yes. Cut these dreads off and pay me my money!"

"How much was this bet worth? You know it's been a year and my memory isn't as good as it used to be!"

"Don't get forgetful now, son! Pay up and shut up fool. Five Hundred big ones."

"Are you sure it was $500 dollars?"

"Yes, I'm positive. I would not have let my hair grow like this for nothing bro'."

"What's got you in such a jolly mood this morning? I almost didn't recognize your voice when you called."

"Well, aside from getting my hair cut and collecting your money, I've met a beautiful woman. She's waiting for me at home, so hurry up."

"Damn! You're finally over that last girl, huh?" Dat's good. I didn't really like her for you! She was up to no good. If this new one has got you smiling, you keep her. It isn't too much of dat going around lately."

"Why? What's up?"

"You remember, Marlon? He used to cut hair here not too long ago."

"Yeah, tall guy, brown skinned."

"Well, he got robbed last week not too far from his house and they shot and killed him."

"Dag, I'm sorry to hear dat. I'll pray for him and his family members."

"Yeah, you do dat. Shit is getting wild out here nowadays."

"Yeah, but you stay up, son. Don't let it get you down. All you can do is pray and trust in God. Life is too short to be down about what's going on out here."

"Yeah, true dat, Kyle, man. You keep smiling and loving your woman. I'll be all done soon. You coming back in a week?"

"Yeah, I'll see you on Saturday. You know, bald men are in now. I got to keep it tight."

"I hear you, go on home to your woman and let her rub on it."

"Yeah, you a fool, man. I'll see you next week!"

"I rushed back home before B. awoke and quietly walked into the bedroom. She was still asleep so, I reached out to caress her face and kissed her forehead. She opened her eyes, and smiled.

Putting my arms around her, I said, "Hey, baby! Did you sleep O.K.?"

"Um. Yes. I slept great!"

"Are you hungry? We could go to brunch, if you'd like."

"Sure, a Sunday brunch sounds good. What time is it?"

"It's 11:00. You looked tired so I let you sleep all morning."

"Where've you been? What happened to your hair?"

"I had it cut this morning. Then, I rushed back to be with you."

"Why'd you rush? I'm not in any hurry to leave."

"It's been along time since a beautiful woman has slept in my bed."

"That's hard to believe?"

"Now, why is that so hard to believe?"

"Kyle, from what I've experienced, you seem to be every woman's dream. You're attractive, dark, tall, bald, and sexy as hell. You also have your own house, car, and business. Women are probably stalking you. You don't have to play any games with me. I'm a grown and intelligent woman. I know the game, baby!"

"If you knew the game so well, Ms. B. Havin, then maybe you'd know that I'm not in it. Yeah, women approach me, but that doesn't mean that I accept what they're offering. I like sex just like the next man, but because I do have myself together, as you so nicely put it, I have to think with my head and not my penis when it comes to who I choose to spend my time with."

"Excuse me! I didn't mean to offend you. I just didn't want you to believe, because I'm young that I was dumb, too! It's just that men try to run that "you're the only woman I see" line on me way too often.

"I'm not offended. However, I have told you that I'm trying to really love you. I know that may be hard for you to believe right now, but I have no interest in playing games with your mind or your heart. I have never nor do I ever have any intentions on being that kind of man."

After that statement, the room grew silent. Bianca and I stared each other, in the eyes for at least five minutes. Then she spoke, "Kyle, I don't think I'm ready for what you're trying to offer me."

"Then, I won't offer it to you right now. I'll back off, and when you think you're ready, you let me know."

"So what will happen with us until then?"

"Well, for starters, we're going to get up and go get breakfast. Afterwards, we'll be friends."

"Kissing friends, I hope!"

"I don't know about all of that."

"Why?"

"I might like it too much."

We hugged and laughed aloud and even though it wasn't what I wanted at the time, we became nothing more than good kissing friends.

BIANCA

THE FRIENDSHIP

In the next two weeks Kyle and I grew closer and closer. I had never experienced a better friendship with anyone else. We shared stories with each other that I would have never shared with Sarah. Kyle was different. Somehow I felt he was warmer and more genuine than any of my other friends. We didn't compete, lie, or intimidate each other as I often felt I did with others. I was glad that I did not take him up on his offer. I felt it would have ruined everything.

During the week, I would go to his restaurant and have dinner with him. We'd sit for hours, drink, and talk about our day and the crazy people we'd come across. It was like I was finally exhaling in front of the fireplace with Whitney Houston, Angela Bassett, and those other two chicks. Nothing like my weekend dates with Tom, Dick, and Harry, Kyle was gentle and patient. He was really interested in what I had to say and what I thought about everyday life events. He was getting to my heart through my mind, not through my panties and I appreciated him for that.

On Thursday night, he called me at home and suggested we eat at another restaurant. He said, "Hey B., why don't you put on that orange dress I bought you and come out with me tonight. I want to do something different today. Let's go to Mexican Village for dinner and then go dancing at the Parabox. I heard it's a great place to learn the Salsa dance."

"That sounds cool, Boo! What time are you going to pick me up?"

"I'm not. We're not dating. Remember? We are just two friends meeting for dinner, and going dancing afterwards."

"Oh! It's like that, huh? That's O.K. Don't trip when all the men want to dance with me."

"I'm not worried about that at all. You better watch all those women who will be trying to feel me up tonight!"

"Yeah right! Where have you been? Women don't do that anymore."

"We'll see! I'll meet you in front of the restaurant about 8:30. Is that cool?"

"Yeah, I'll be there."

I hung up the phone and began to look through my closet for the orange silk Versace dress that he was referring to, but it wasn't there. I knew I had picked up all of my things from the cleaners on Monday. I wondered if those Chinese women stole my dress or messed up and put it on someone else's order. If that was the case I was going to be heated. I began to formulate the tongue-lashing I was going to give those broads in the morning. Then it occurred to me that it was probably in Sarah's closet. She had a bad habit of borrowing my clothes without my permission.

I walked down the hall and quietly knocked on her door. "Hey Sarah! You got my orange dress in there?" When I didn't hear a response I pushed the door open and went in. Her room was a mess. Talking to myself, I walked toward the closet.

"I don't know how you find anything in this junky ass room!" I was truly hoping that if she did have my shit it was hanging up in the closet. I stepped over a few pairs of shoes and opened the sliding doors to the closet.

"Thank you Sarah for telling me you borrowed my dress. I hope you don't have my shoes in this bitch too! Oh! I see that you do. I need to start borrowing your stuff so freely. If my shit is musty you are going to pay for the cleaning this time."

As I turned to leave the pigsty, I noticed two bags of weed on her dresser. "This girl is getting out of hand with this shit. First, it was a joint here and there, now it's everyday. She better have her part of the rent this month or her ass is out."

I got dressed in under an hour, curled my hair, and called Kyle to let him know I would meet him on time. I had been late a few times in the past, so he made me promise to call him whenever we decided to meet up to let him know if I would be on time or not. He answered on the second ring. "Yeah, this is Kyle."

"I know this is Kyle. I'm on my way and I'm on time!"

"Alright, I'll see you in a minute."

We each hung up our cell phones and I started out to the parking garage. I pushed the elevator button and played with my hair one last time in the mirror in the lobby. "My hair is not going to last tonight." When the doors opened I got in with two other women, spoke, and asked one of them to "push three please!" The elevator door opened and I walked to my car. It was in its usual spot on the end of the second row, but it looked different. As I got closer, my mouth fell open in disbelief. My front windows were knocked out and two of my tires were flat. "What the fuck?" I couldn't believe what I was seeing. I ran up closer to read what was written on the windshield. In big red letters was written the word "Whore!"

I stuck my hand down in my purse and grabbed my pocketknife and my cell phone. I cautiously looked around my surroundings and dialed the police. Then I walked down to the security guard's booth and knocked on his window. The fat bastard was sleeping with headphones on so I banged on the windows and screamed, "Wake your fat ass up, Benny!" He jumped at the sound of his name and apologized for snoozing on the job. "You just ought to apologize. My car has been vandalized and you didn't even catch the guy who did it."

Needless to say, I was going to be late for my date with Kyle. I called him back and told him what happened. He was surprised that no one saw the incident. I told the police about my phone call with Steve. He was the only person I could think of that would want to do such a thing. I hadn't slept with, or gone out with, anyone since I'd met Kyle so I didn't think it was a scorned girlfriend. I filed a police report and called the insurance company. Being the good friend he was, Kyle insisted that I take his Lexus. He would drive the rental car while my car was being repaired. He really knew how to spoil me.

We decided not to cancel our plans for the evening over such nonsense. We went to the restaurant together and then we cut a rug at the Latino club. It was easy for me to forget all of my troubles when I was with him. Afterward, we went back to his place. I showered and called Sarah to tell her I wouldn't be home, but I didn't get an answer. I left her a message and warmed up my leftovers in Kyle's microwave. "Hey Kyle! Do you want any of this before I devour it?"

"No, you go ahead. I'm going to get in the shower and turn in. You know where everything is. Will you be O.K.?"

"I guess so. I'm going to watch a little T.V. then I'll come and get in the bed," hoping he wouldn't catch on to that last statement.

"What do you mean? Don't you think you should sleep out here since we're just good friends? This isn't like the first time you stayed here. I'm not giving up my bed for you today. My back hurts and my feet are tired. You stepped on them all night. My friends sleep on the couch. My woman sleeps in my bed."

"I wasn't your woman two weeks ago."

"No, you weren't, but back then I wanted you to be, so it was O.K. for me to be a gentleman and give you my bed. Now that you have made it clear that we are just going to be friends, you no longer have that privilege."

The microwave buzzer beeped to let me know that my food was warmed, but I ignored it. The four margaritas I'd consumed were still working on me and I was horny. So, I seductively walked over to Kyle and opened my gown. We both knew that I wanted to have sex with him from day one. I admit that I had been holding back for the last two weeks with respect to his wishes, but he did say for me to let him know when I was ready for what he had to offer. I enjoyed our friendship true enough, but I really wanted to know just how good his lovemaking would be.

"So, are you saying that you don't want me now? You mean to tell me that you would make me sleep on that old couch." Caressing his chess with my fingertips," What if I rubbed your back and kissed your feet? Do you think I could sleep in your bed again?"

"Bianca, what are you doing?" Getting serious, "You know that I will always want you. The question is, do you want me?"

"Yes, very much."

"I'm not talking about one night B. Are you saying that you are ready to be in a committed relationship with me?"

Pressing my body against his and kissing his lips, "Kyle, I'm saying that I want to feel you inside of me right now."

Kissing my forehead softly and pulling me in closer, he whispered in my ear, "No, Bianca. I want you to be all mine when we make love and not before then. If you would just say those words to me I would make love to you over and over again."

"Yes, Kyle. I'm yours baby. I'm yours. Now please, make love to me!"

Feeling his penis rise, I unbuttoned his pants and we kissed passionately. He picked me up in his muscular arms and sat me on the cold marble kitchen counter. Then he took each one of my full breasts in his hands and sucked each nipple. I did not resist when he slid my thong down my thighs and dropped to his knees to taste my wet vagina. I screamed his name as I grabbed the back of his bald head and climaxed in his mouth. We then moved to the floor, where he thrust his erect penis inside of me. It was more than I could have ever imagined. Just when I thought I was going to reach my mountaintop again, he pulled out and let his hot semen spread across my stomach.

I was surprised that in a matter of five minutes I had just had the most incredible sex ever. It was a little disappointing that it didn't last longer. However, I was flattered. I was always told that, when a man comes fast, he is really turned on by you.

BIANCA

One week had gone by since the night we slept together and Kyle and I were closer than two peas in a pod. We would call each other every day, talk for hours and hang out every weekend. I know that I had told him that I was ready to be his, but we both knew that was just for that one moment. I wanted sex and he wanted to hear those words. Deep down, we both knew that we were meant to be together, but we also knew that I wasn't ready. I needed to be sure that my relationship with Kyle would not be a repeat of the time I wasted with Chauncey. I also needed to be sure that the freak in me was ready to slow down as well. If and when I did decide to settle down with Kyle I wanted to be honest and true to him. He deserved to have a good woman just as he felt I deserved to have a good man. I had to learn to cut my old ties and shut the door to my closet of tricks.

I went into the kitchen and poured a glass of wine. As I sipped the chilled beverage, I walked to the couch and turned on the radio with the remote. It was 11:00 at night and WJLB, the R&B

radio station, was playing Stephanie Mill's "Power of Love." I pushed the volume button to fill the apartment with her strong cords. Then, I chimed in, "I've learned to respect, the power of love.. I need you... I want you beside me... I trust you... Ooh I believe in you... I adore you... I love you soooo. Let's talk about the loving Oooh... Oooh. Let's talk about the feeling. Let's talk about the yearning Oooh... Oooh." When the song ended, I continued with the chorus and I sang until I was hoarse and tears ran down my face.

When I realized how silly I looked, dancing around my apartment, I turned the music down and laughed as hard as I could and it felt GREAT! It was then that I realized, for the first time, in a long time, that I was deliriously happy. I felt like I had the love that Stephanie was screaming about and I was sitting on top of the world.

So, why was I being the complete idiot for making my joy wait for me? Kyle was a wonderful man and I was pushing him away by playing games and lying to myself. I didn't want this other bullshit out here in the street. I wanted to be loved, nurtured, and adored. I wanted the unconditional love that the singers sang about. I wanted the shit that the movies portrayed to be strong and forever undying. I wanted Kyle Sinclair. I loved every thing about that man. His touch made me shiver, his smile made me quiver, and his sweet and gentle kisses made the seat of my panties moist each and every time our lips connected. I was fooling myself to believe that I still wanted to be in the dating game. I didn't want to sleep around with any of the losers I was seeing. Kyle's sex was excellent and I wanted it all to myself. I wanted a commitment.

I looked over at the clock on the VCR and saw that it was well past midnight. But, I wanted to rush to him and let him know that I was ready. I knew it was late, but we'd stayed up plenty of nights until one and two o'clock talking on the phone. So, I was sure he'd be awake. I grabbed my coat, keys, and purse and rushed over to his house.

It wasn't until I had reached my exit on the freeway that I'd realized that I didn't have a clue as to how I would approach Kyle. I thought about rehearsing some corny line, but decided against it. Then, I thought I'd just greet him with a kiss and blurt out "I love you, Kyle with all my heart and I'm ready to start the rest of our lives together." Then, I bit my bottom lip, which is a bad habit I picked up during my teenage years. "Damn! What do I say? How can I do this?" I wasn't familiar with this shit. This was all brand new to me. Men usually approached me with this silly shit. I never had to approach them nor do I know how to!

"Bianca," I said aloud, "Turn this car around and take your crazy ass home. Think this love shit through and then call him tomorrow." So, that's exactly what I did and as I unlocked the door to my apartment, I laughed aloud and said, "This guy really has you going huh?" I unbuttoned my coat and kicked off my shoes. I got undressed, fell in the bed, and stared at the ceiling until I fell asleep.

KYLE

"I rubbed the temples of my head and I watched the waitress pour the steaming black coffee into the ceramic coffee cups. I had called my best friend, Mike, and had him meet me at the Dunkin Donuts near my house. I needed someone to talk to. He and I had been through a lot together and he was the only one of my friends who knew what it was like to be in love."

"So what's up man? Your phone call sounded urgent."

"Bianca has become a very special part of my life over the last few months, man. She is what I think of first thing in the morning. What I long for in the afternoon and what I have prayed for and dreamed about every night. It's obvious that I love her. However, I'm getting tired of her distrust and fear of letting me into her heart. I have proven myself to her time and time again. Yet, she continues to resist what I'm trying to offer her."

"Man, what in the hell are you talking about?"

"We made love man, and I'm ready to commit. I went without touching another woman since Tamara for eight months and then Bianca came along and knocked me off my block. But it's not just about sex with her, I really want to be with her. Man, I called her late last night to set things up, but she wasn't home. I'm sure it's because she was on another date."

"Damn, man! This girl has got your ass twisted. Have you told her how you feel?"

"No, I didn't want to mess things up by telling her that I want to marry her right away. She's special."

"Maybe if you'd tell her and lay the dick down, she wouldn't keep giving up the pussy to these other dudes."

"Naw, she's not like that anymore. I don't think she's sleeping with them."

"What do you mean you don't think she's fucking them? How do you know?"

"Man, I've been dating her, too and we have only made love once, but I could tell she hadn't had any in a while."

"Then what is the problem? I'm saying call dat girl, tell her exactly how you feel. Man what? Do dat shit already!"

"Naw, man. She has to come to me! Bianca knows exactly how I feel about us. I'm just afraid that when she's ready for the same thing, I won't be there for her any longer. I'm ready to move on! One minute she says she's ready, we sleep together, and then she's unsure again. The sex is the bomb, but I want more. Tracy called last night and says she wants to go out with me. So, I'm taking her to the comedy club tonight. I think she wants to get with me."

"Tracy? Is that the skinny girl from church? Man, are you out of your mind? That girl is the last person you need to be spending money or time with. She's crazy!"

"She's not crazy. She's just a little different. Besides, it beats sitting around waiting on B."

"Your ass must want some head or something. That's all dat is. You just tired of waiting. Let's keep the shit real here."

"Yeah, you're right. I don't want to be with Tracy."

"What are you going to tell B. when she finds out you're dating again?"

"We're just friends, I don't have to explain anything to her. If she can date other men, I can date other women!"

"Are you sure you want to do that?"

"No, but maybe this will be an eye opener for her. She needs to know that she can't keep me on the back burner forever."

"Alright then Kyle, do dat shit. But if it back fires on your ass, don't say I didn't warn you."

Mike and I finished our breakfast and went our separate ways. When I crossed the street to get to my car, he was still standing in front of the bakery flirting with a tall brunette. It was good seeing Mike again. Our talk really helped me come to grips with my situation with Bianca. When I drove pass the two, I honked my horn and threw up a peace sign.

BIANCA

The alarm clock read 12:45 p.m. when my bladder woke me from the comatose sleep I'd fallen into the night before. I jumped out of the bed and raced past Sarah to the bathroom.

"Whoa! Girl, what's wrong with you?"

"Nothing, I just had to pee. Where've you been? I haven't seen you in days."

"Honey, you're not the only one who can sleep around you know! Sarah's got a man too!"

"Oh yeah! Who's the man?" I yelled through the closed bathroom door.

"His name is David. He's a male dancer at Henry's Palace.

Talking over the flushing toilet, "He's a what? Girl, you know you are crazy! Is he cute? How many kids does he have? Where does he live and why didn't you tell me about him before you decided to stay out with him for days?"

"Yes, he's cute. That's the only way I like them. He doesn't have any children and he lives ten minutes away. I've been coming home daily. You just haven't been here when I was!"

"Um!" I grunted, while brushing my teeth.

"Hey! What's up with you and Steve? He's been calling here a lot lately? Are you two an item again? What happened to Kyle?"

I dried my face with my towel and rolled my eyes to the ceiling as if she could see me. "Girl!" Opening the bathroom door, "That fool is a crazy bastard! I told him to stop calling me!"

"Steve?"

"Yes, Steve's punk ass! He's a pain in my ass! He won't leave me the hell alone."

"Well, he sounded a little upset when I told him you weren't in, but I didn't think to much of it."

"So what, if he's upset! I'm upset, too!"

"What's up with Kyle? Are you two an official couple yet?"

Reaching in her plate to steal a piece of bacon, "No, not yet!"

"Does that mean you two are getting closer?"

Giggling, I hesitated to respond before I disclosed my actions of last night. "Hah! Girl you are a mess. So someone has finally captured your wild ass, huh?"

"I guess you could say that. I haven't told him how I feel yet. He might not want me anymore. I mean I have been putting him off for a week now. I don't even know how to approach him with this. What if he's moved on and given up on me?"

"You won't know until you talk to him. But, I'm almost certain he hasn't I've seen the way he looks at you. He hangs on your every word and is hypnotized by the way you move. He's whipped!"

I poured myself a glass of milk. "No he's not,

and I can tell he's getting tired of waiting on me. He's been acting different."

"Damn. Maybe I was wrong. When are you going to call him?"

"Maybe a little later. I'm going to the gym to work out. I might do a few laps in the pool, too!"

"Want some company?"

"Sure, you can tell me all about this new guy while I jog around you on the track."

"Yeah, right!" Stretching her legs, "You mean as I jog around you?"

"Does he have a brother? I might need a back up plan if Kyle turns me away!"

"Actually, he does, a twin brother, in fact!"

"Are you serious? What's his name? What does he do?"

"Donald, and he's a dancer too! He warms up the crowd a little before the other guys come out. I think I'll set something up. Maybe we can double date before you and Kyle decide to tie the knot."

"I don't want to double date. You know I like to keep my shit undercover."

"Yeah, I know you do! Freak!"

"Yeah that's me! You wish you could be one, too!"

We gave each other a high five, hugged, and then mocked Martin Lawrence, "Girl, you so crazy!"

"Let's go before I change my mind and go get back to my bed."

BIANCA

The bathroom clock read 8:05 p.m. when I got out of the shower. I wiped some of the hot steam from a corner of the mirror, and began to floss my teeth. My wet hair stuck to my face as I plucked the leftover red meat from each crevice. Sarah and I had stopped at the steak house down the street on the way home. They have wonderful T-bones and loaded baked potatoes. I ordered a tossed salad and a glass of wine to accompany the main course while my roommate opted for a beer. We talked and laughed out loud about our ex-boyfriends and some of the riff raff that had entered the restaurant. However, I would frequently drift into my own world and daydream about Kyle. I was curious about what it would be like to be married to him. His hands were always so gentle, and his lips were full and wet. I started to reminisce his kissing me all over and making me explode.

Tonight was definitely going to be the night that I shared my feelings and made passionate love with him again. I'd planned on showing up at his door with nothing but a trench coat and heels.

However, Sarah thought that was a boring idea. She jokingly said, "Everyone does that B. You should go in your bra and panties and wear my yellow Nautica jacket with your yellow and white gym shoes. That would be more original!" Then, she insisted that I wear my sexy halter cut cat suit and matching thong. I agreed and rushed to get dressed.

Once I'd modeled in front of the mirror two or three times, I decided to call him to say that I was on my way, but Sarah was on the phone making plans for the evening with her new beau. The clock now read 9:30 so I pulled out my cell phone and dialed his number. I was very disappointed when his voice mail service requested that I leave a message at the sound of the tone.

"Shit!" I slammed the phone down.

Putting her hands over the receiver, "Girl, what's wrong with you?"

"He's gone out. He's not home!"

"I'm sorry B. Did you leave a message?"

"No! I can't tell the man I love him on a voice mail message. I wanted to tell him in person and see his expression."

"Well, you could always go out with me and David tonight and call him tomorrow. We're going down to the comedy club on Jefferson. I hear that crazy female comedian, Co Co, will be there tonight."

"Naw girl! I don't want to be a third wheel with you and your new guy."

Talking into the phone, "What honey?" Pause.

"B., David says he can get his brother to come and keep you company if you want."

"How can I go out with his brother tonight and confess my love to Kyle tomorrow, Sarah? That's crazy!"

"No, it's coming out and having fun with a group of friends. Nobody said you had to sleep with this guy. Just have a few drinks and laugh Bianca, damn! We haven't double dated in a long time girl, come on."

"Aw'right I'll go. But I'm driving my own car. Maybe I can catch up with Kyle afterwards."

"Cool! Honey, she said she'd come. Bring Donald with you when you pick me up."

When Sarah hung up the phone, I tried Kyle's house again and still there was no answer. "This doesn't feel right. Kyle usually lets me know when he's going out with his friends. I hope everything is O.K."

"Stop worrying. He's a grown man. He's O.K. Maybe he didn't go out with friends. Maybe he's with another woman."

"What other woman? Kyle only has eyes for me. There is no other woman."

"Yeah, O.K. Bianca. That's what you said about Chauncey's punk ass, too. Remember?"

"Kyle is different, Sarah. He's nothing like my ex. You even said you thought he was sprung on me. He wouldn't hurt me like that."

"Hurt you like what B.? You've been going out with other men and stringing him along for a month. You said yourself that you've been pushing him away. Why would you be hurt if he's out with someone else now? Technically, he's a free man. He can date whomever he wants when he wants. It's selfish of you to date other people and expect him to just wait and not see anyone else."

"He told me that he wasn't interested in seeing anyone else Sarah. I didn't ask him to wait for me, I just assumed he would."

"Well you know what they say about assumptions."

"Yeah you make an ass out of you and me."

"Don't sweat it girl. Just come on out with us tonight and call him on your lunch break tomorrow."

"I'm cool. I am not trippin." I just hope you haven't hooked me up with any bullshit tonight, girl! Are these guys cute? You know I can't be seen out wit no ugly ass man."

"Trust me! You're going to be glad you didn't commit yourself to Kyle tonight. These brothers are fine. They do a routine together down at the dick bar and they have all the women throwing their money at them."

"Well, I don't know nothing about giving no man my money, but I might damn sure give him some pussy if Kyle is out with another woman."

"Girl, stop it!"

BIANCA

"I cannot believe how cold it is tonight?"

"Yeah, I know. Do you want to come closer? Maybe our body heat could keep us warm."

"No, I'm fine. I just hope we don't have much longer to wait in this stupid line. Sarah, why didn't you come down here earlier to buy the tickets? It's cold as hell out here. I'm mad they make people wait outside to buy tickets for this shit."

"Bianca, chill out. This wasn't a planned event; we just decided to come here at 8:30. You should've worn a bigger jacket."

"Let's trade, you let me wear yours and I'll give you mine."

"Yeah right! Why would I do that?"

"You and David can hug each other. He can open his jacket and let you in. It's big enough."

"I offered to share mine with you, baby."

"No thanks, Donald."

"O.K. It's your call."

I cannot believe I let Sarah talk me into this double date shit. David and Donald were both two skinny funny ass-looking dudes who thought they were God's gift to women. They both wore identical Coogi sweaters and pants that were two sizes too big. The only thing sexy about them was their big ass wet lips, but even that was a turn off after Donald kept giving me wet kisses on my face and the backs of each hand. Why do men always have to come on so strong? He was too far into my personal space. I should've waited at home until Kyle answered his phone. I should've waited outside his house in my car until he got there. Anything would've been better than standing out here knee deep in this bullshit fighting off this loser.

Sarah spoke, "Hey, the line is moving again!"

"Good, maybe we can get close enough to the door to feel the heat!" I responded.

"You sure are trippin' tonight, Bianca. Calm yo' ass down please!"

"You're right girl, I am trippin'. I should've just stayed home."

Donald mumbled, "That's exactly what I was thinkin'."

"Hey, look over there in the valet line. Doesn't that look like Kyle's car?"

"Oh! Now you're hallucinating."

"No really, I think that's his car. Can you see if he's still in it?"

"No I can't see anything."

Turning to David, Sarah said, "Baby, can you tell if anyone is in that white Lexus truck up there?"

"Uh, no there's no one in it. Why?"

"My girl thinks that is her friend's ride."

"Oh! She's into dudes like that, huh! Baby, $100 says my brother can hit it better than that guy."

"Your brother couldn't hit this shit for $1000."

"You're a funny acting bitch, you know. My brother came out tonight as a favor to me because yo' ass was at home alone. All you've done is complain since we've got here. He's not having any more fun than you are right now. So you need to check yourself. You aren't all dat!"

Just as I was about to tell this rude arrogant ass man how I really felt about him and his sorry ass brother, the line moved again. Sarah caught my arm and pulled me along with her. "Sarah, he does not know me like that!"

"No, Bianca, he's right. We came out to have fun tonight and you're ruining it for all of us. Let's just go in, listen to these jokes, and chill."

"Alright, I'm sorry, David, Donald, and Sarah. But," turning to David, "I do suggest that you rethink it before you call me another bitch."

We all laughed and Donald put his arm around me as we stepped inside the club. The owner had to have the heat on hell inside the corridor. There was a cute, petite woman with long hair standing behind a table checking everyone's I.D. "You must be 21 with proper identification young lady." Showing her my license, "Thanks! I'll take that as a compliment." Donald looked down at the picture after she'd given it back to me. "You do look pretty young."

"You think so?"

"Yeah, I do. I also think you're very sexy. I'm surprised you were home alone tonight. Why would any woman as beautiful as you be waiting at home on a man. I'd take you out and show you off everyday if you were my lady."

"Thank you. You're not so bad yourself. I'm surprised there isn't a lady at home waiting for you."

"Well, there is one, my wife, Sheree. She's there with my three kids."

"What?"

"No, I'm kidding! I only have two kids."

"And a wife?"

"No, I'm joking. There's no wife, just my two kids. I'm just a single dad out here working and dating."

"So what's it like being a male dancer?"

"It's fun. I get to travel and meet a lot of women."

"Sarah said you were a firefighter also. How do you do both?"

"No, I'm not a firefighter. Maybe she got confused with my stage name."

"Oh! What's your stage name?"

Licking his big ass lips, smiling, and pulling out my chair, "The Fire Fighter, 'cause I like to put out the hot ladies' fire. But, that's enough about me. Tell me something about you."

"Well, my life isn't nearly as exciting as yours."

"Oh! Now you going to act like that?"

"No, I'm just kidding. I'm really sorry for the way I acted before. Let me buy you a drink."

"It's cool, don't sweat it. Let me buy you a drink. You just promise not to be so uptight all night."

"It's a deal. I'll have a Corona with a lime."

"I'll be right back. Eh! Dave you and your girl want anything from the bar?"

Donald took their orders and excused himself from the table. Sarah and I held a little small talk about some of the hoochies and busters as they walked by our table, but she paid more attention to David than me. I took the hint, closed my eyes, and began tapping my feet, and humming along to the Mary J. Blidge tune the DJ was playing.

When Donald returned with our drinks, the lights were dimmed and the DJ announced the first comedian. I opened my eyes, smiled, retrieved my drink and said thanks. It seemed he was a nice guy after all. I was even beginning to think he was cute. When he pulled out his chair to sit down I took it upon myself to check out what Mr. Firefighter was working with. When he caught me staring I was a little embarrassed, but he put his arm around me, pulled me close, and said "I'd be more than happy to give you a better view later." I smiled and patted him on the leg. "No thanks."

"Well, you started it!"

"Shh! You two!!" Sarah whispered across the table. "I don't want to bring any unnecessary attention to our table. You know these comedians like to clown people up front."

"Well, shut up then!" I whispered back.

The plus sized woman on the stage started out by saying hello to all the beautiful black people in the audience. Then she commented on how sexy all the men were and received a few cheers from the anxious crowd. The hair on the back of my neck stood up, when she started in on jokes about all the skinny women in the crowd. I thought for sure she would comment on how small I looked in my tight fitting cat suit, I crossed my fingers and said a silent prayer when she turned toward our side of the room. Something told me to get up and go to the bathroom when she pointed in my direction, but I thought that might bring more attention to me. I reached down and grabbed Donald's hand and clenched my teeth.

"Look at her up there with that red miniskirt."

I exhaled as the stage crew put a bright spot light on a young and attractive lady two tables behind ours. "Thank God, she didn't notice me." Donald and Sarah giggled, as we all turned around to catch a view of the comic's victim. "That girl so skinny, her thong probably looks like a full cotton brief. Sitting up there with that big sexy ass man. What are you going to do wit that skinny girl? You need to get a big girl in your life, 'cause we know how to treat a big man. See me after the show and give me yo' number. Eh! Somebody take that man a drink on me."

My stomach did twenty flips in the two seconds it took me to recognize that the big attractive gentleman the comedian was referring to was my Kyle. He put his arm around the young lady and pulled her close to save her from the embarrassment and to console her feelings. Before I knew it, I'd thrown up all over Donald's shoes. That caused a big commotion in our section and the big spotlight was then placed on my table. The comedian then went on to say, "Damn, what did she drink? Don't give me or my new man over there any of that shit!"

The crowd was hysterical. Everyone was laughing at me. I felt like that crazy girl, Carrie, in that old 80s movie. So, I jumped up and ran outside of the club and didn't look behind. When I got out front, I sat on the ground and vomited again. Sarah, David, and Donald, came out about a minute later and helped me up.

"Bianca, are you O.K.? I'm sorry you saw that."

"Saw what?" Donald questioned.

"That was her friend in their with that girl."

"Oh! Damn. I'm sorry too."

"No, I'm fine now. Really, you guys go back in, I'll come back in soon. I just needed some fresh air."

"Naw, B. I saw the look on your face when Kyle was all hugged up with that girl. You shouldn't be here. We can all go somewhere else."

"No, it's cool. Like you said earlier, he's not my man. He can date whomever! I don't want to ruin everyone's night out."

"Hey! Why don't I take you somewhere else and Sarah and my brother can go back inside.

"Bianca, you're not messing up our evening.

That girl wasn't that funny. We can all leave if you want."

"No, Sarah. I'll let Donald drive me home in my car. You two can stay. Please. I'll be O.K."

"Alright girl, but if you need me just call my cell phone. I won't stay out late, I'll come home as soon as the show ends, O.K."

"Don't worry about me, really."

Sarah and I hugged before she and David went back inside. Donald handed me a few leftover Kleenex tissues he'd had after cleaning off his shoe. "Are you really O.K. Bianca? Let me help you to the car."

"Thanks Donald. I was just really taken by surprise to see him in there with someone else. That's just the kind of stuff you see on T.V. I've never been played that way in my life,"

"Well, it happens to the best of us. You'll be O.K. though. Think of it this way, he saw you with me too. So, he's hurt just like you are."

"You think so?"

"Yeah, that girl was not all of that. Her weave weighed more than she did."

"Thanks, Donnie. I needed that."

"So you want to go for a ride through Belle Isle before I take you home?"

"Yeah! That sounds cool."

BIANCA

Donnie opened up the passenger side of my car and made sure I was in before closing the door. I leaned over and unlocked the driver's side so he didn't have to stand in the cold too long. He started the engine and put the heat dial on high. I unbuttoned my coat and slipped my shoes off as not to get overheated. Donald reached out to turn on the radio and then gently caressed my face. I nibbled at the back of his hand playfully before I intertwined our fingers and placed his hand in my lap.

"So, Mr. Firefighter, I guess it's just you and me tonight, huh?"

"Does that bother you? Being alone with me like this?"

"No, not at all. I've had plenty of first dates. This is my first blind date, though."

"So, what do you think? Would you go out on a second date with me?"

"Yes. I didn't think so at first, but I was trippin' earlier. You actually turned out to be a nice guy. I'm also dying to see you dance for me."

"Do you want me to take my clothes off, too?"

"I wouldn't have it any other way! I want the whole show!"

"Do you have your dollar bills ready?"

"Yes sir!"

"Girl, you're funny. I will not let you use me as the rebound guy."

"Donnie, I would never do that. I was just making conversation. I didn't mean it like that."

"No, Bianca, I know you didn't. I was just joking. I would be whatever you wanted me to be, when you wanted me to be. It's cool."

He pulled the car over and parked under a giant tree. "Do you know how to ballroom?"

"Well, I'm no professional but, I can dance a little bit."

"You up for it?"

"Out here? Are you crazy?"

"Come on girl. It'll be fun."

I put my shoes on and climbed out into the chilly night air. We left the car windows down and turned the radio up as high as it would go. Donnie grabbed my hand, ran out into the street, and then pulled me in close to his warm hard body. This man was definitely beginning to turn me on. We danced for three songs and laughed each time I stepped on his shoes. He made me feel real good after the nightmare I'd experienced at the comedy club an hour earlier.

"I love your smile Bianca."

"Yours isn't so bad either Donnie."

"Thanks! You know I'm real sorry about what happened tonight. I'd like to take your mind off of it completely. That happened to me once and I was trippin' for months afterwards."

"Oh! Yeah! What happened?"

"It's a long story. Let's just say I got played."

"How'd you get over it?"

"You know, my friends and my brother brought me out of it. We hung out, drank, and smoked. And..." swinging me out for my solo performance before finishing his statement, "played with my PlayStation II."

Trying to look smooth, I pranced around a little and stopped to do an imitation of Beyonce's booty dance, but I slipped and fell. Laughing, he rushed to my assistance and gently pulled me to my feet.

"Damn, heels!"

Leaning in, Donald said, "May I kiss you?"

I smiled, "Yes, you may."

As our lips parted our tongues began to dance to their own tune. My arms wrapped themselves around his neck and my body was under his spell. He carried me back to the car, rolled the windows up, and pulled on the zipper to my outfit. I held onto the side of his face and watched the top of his head wriggle between my breasts. I moaned with pleasure as he rubbed the inside of my thighs and vagina. When he kissed me again, my lips parted and I thought to myself, those big ass lips that I'd complained about earlier had actually turned out to be a Godsend. He had definitely made me feel better. I'd never been fingered like that before. I closed my eyes a rested my head on the headrest. The foggy windows and our loud panting sounds, drowned out all of the outside noises and we did not notice the cop car that had pulled up behind us. We both pulled our jackets over my body when the police officer knocked on the window and turned on his flashlight. I thought we were going to be in a world of trouble.

"Can I see some I.D. please?"

"Damn! A completely terrific moment, ruined."

BIANCA

"What! Girl, what happened then?" Sarah questioned the next day.

"Well, the policeman was cool. He gave us a ticket for loitering in the park after it had closed an told us to leave."

Sarah began to yell, "Oh! My goodness. You two are so bad! Maybe Kyle wasn't the man you were supposed to be with after all. Maybe Donnie is Mr. Lover man. I know David is my soul mate. Hey! Maybe we can have a double wedding."

I told her, "No, I don't think so. Pump your breaks honey, pump your breaks."

"Huh?"

I told her to slow down! I said, "The attention and affection felt good. I didn't say he was marriage material. You know there is a difference. I believe if more people knew this, there would be fewer divorced and unhappy people."

Agreeing, surprisingly, Sarah said, "You're right. Some relationships should just remain sexual. Marriage does complicate things."

"No, that's not what I'm saying. Marriage is a wonderful thing if a couple is truly in love with one another. It's the sex that complicates things. When I get married, I want to know that if, God forbid, something ever happened to me, something that prevented me from having sex, my husband would still stand by me through sickness and health, richer or poorer."

"So then, we're back on Kyle. Are you going to call him?" Sarah probed.

"Yeah, I think I am. He's probably angry with me too, for being there with Donnie. So, I want to call and explain my side of the story."

"What about letting him call you and explaining his side."

"Sarah, Kyle is the man that I intend to keep, forever. He has already shown me how much he cares for me. Now, it's my turn. He didn't do anything wrong. Neither of us did. I want to clear the slate. I'm going to call him, be honest, tell the truth, and ask that we start over."

"Are you sure you want to do that? You did say Donald's sex might be the bomb! He's a dancer - you know he'll be freaky!"

"Yeah, but I'm sure Kyle is who I want to be with."

RING... RING... RING

"Do you think that's Kyle?"

"I don't know. Maybe you should answer the phone and see. No wait, what am I saying, racing to the phone. I'll answer it."

"Now, who needs to slow down? Damn girl! Try not to sound so anxious."

Giving her the finger, I fumbled with the

cordless phone. Then in my sexiest voice, "Hello!"

"Yeah, is this Bianca?"

"Yes it is. May I ask who this is?"

"Yeah, bitch, this is Steve. I got a letter in the mail saying that you filed a police report on me. I've been trying to call you to let your dumb ass know that I have better things to do with my time than to vandalize your shit. I've been watching you though and I saw your skank ass out with that dude in the park last night. When can I get my turn? You still playing, "hard to get," with me, huh? That's O.K. though, because the next time I see you out alone, I'm going to take it, TRICK!"

"What the..." Before I could attempt to respond, the other end of the line went dead. "Oh! My God, Sarah! That dude is crazy."

"Who?"

"Steve. He followed us last night and he just threatened to rape me!"

"B. calm down. What did he say?"

"He said he saw me and Donnie at the park and that he was going to rape me the next time I go out alone."

"B. we've got to call the police. That motherfucker has been calling here for a few weeks now."

"The police are going to think this is all my fault. There's no telling how long he's been following me."

"I'm going to call David. Maybe he can let us keep his piece over here."

"No, Sarah! Are you crazy? I don't want a gun

in our house."

"Well B. we can't just sit here and be scared. We have to at least file a police report or something. Damn!"

"O.K., Sarah, calm down. You are starting to make me freak out. I can play this motherfucker's game, too. I'll show him a stalker." I picked up the phone and dialed *69.

"Hello, Steve!"

"Yeah?"

"You have truly fucked with the wrong bitch, now. You know, two can play these games."

"What?"

"You must be the biggest loser ever. You don't have shit better to do than to call and follow me around. Well, yeah, it's on now! If I were you, I'd watch my back."

When I hung up the phone, Sarah looked at me and laughed. "Was he scared B?"

"I don't know and didn't give him a chance to respond."

"Now what are you going to do?"

"Grab your coat and get your car keys. We're going for a ride."

Sarah and I drove to Steve's house on the west side of town. I parked in front of his neighbor's driveway. Then, we got out, crept up on his ride, flattened his tires, scratched the paint, and threw a brick in the windshield. When Steve opened his front door, he was heated.

"What the... I'm calling the police bitch!"

"Good. When they get here I can tell them all

about you following me around. I can also play back your threatening phone call you dumb motherfucker. I taped you." A few of his neighbors were peeping out of their windows. Some were even beginning to come out on their porches to see what all the chaos was about.

"Oh! Look, Boo! Now your neighbors can hear all about it, too! Excuse me, sir?" Walking toward a man standing near the curb, "Did you know Steve was a wannabee stalker? Watch your wife and kids. He said he was going to rape me."

"Bianca shut the fuck up and get off my lawn. Are you crazy?"

"Hell yeah, you bastard! I am, and don't you forget it. Remember dat shit the next time you decide to call my house again!"

When Sarah and I turned to return to her car, the police were coming around the corner. One of his neighbors must have called them. "Shit!" My first instinct said to run, but I didn't feel like I had anything to run away from. Steve basically assaulted me. So I stopped and waited for the police to park and ask me some questions. Steve ran up on us as the police were putting the handcuffs on and yelled, "I want to press full charges on this whore, officers!" The officers pushed him aside and asked him to calm down, but Steve kept insisting. "No! This tramp came to my house and embarrassed me in front of all of my neighbors. I was about to whoop her ass when you two showed up." Once again the police asked him, "Step aside, sir, please!"

Sarah was crying and screaming, "Please officers don't arrest my girl!" The whole scene was very traumatic, but I held my composure. That is until, Steve pushed the policeman who was reading my rights, grabbed me by the neck and said, "I hope your trick ass rots in jail!" Then, it was on. The policeman caught his balance, stepped up, punched him in the nose and pushed him to the ground. The other cop who was talking to the neighbors ran over and assisted as he handcuffed Steve. "Now, you're both going to jail buddy." I laughed, "Now who's going to rot in jail BITCH!"

BIANCA

I told Sarah to call Kyle and my mom when we got to the police station. She followed close behind the police car and almost got arrested, too. I knew my mom would be frantic when she heard the news, but she knew this was not out of character for me. When I was sixteen, I fought a girl inside a music store at the mall, followed her outside, ran my car into hers, and totaled it. She was so disappointed in me, but I was hers and she loved me. Besides, I got it honest. I once witnessed her stab one of her boyfriends after he'd slapped her because she didn't have dinner ready for him on time.

Needless to say, Sarah didn't call Kyle as I'd asked. She called David and Donald instead. They both rushed down to the station. I had to spend a few hours in jail, but Steve decided not to press charges against me because he had more problems to deal with after he'd hit the policeman.

Two days had gone by since I'd seen Kyle at the club and I had not heard from him. So, Donnie and I became much closer after the jail time incident. He was cool. He enjoyed being with what he thought was a 'down ass chick.' He started spending a lot of time at our apartment with his brother, which I thought was a little annoying at times, but it was better than being alone. I missed Kyle. We were both being stubborn. He wouldn't call me, and I didn't call him. I was miserable without him, but I held my ground. Besides, my mom always said, "The best way to get over a man is to get under another one!"

So, the twins, Sarah, and I became a foursome. Meaning, we did a lot of double dating. We went to the movies, the mall and a few clubs when we wanted to dance and get a few drinks. That is, when the guys weren't shaking their asses on stage for other chicks. I believe that was the only thing that kept me from having real feelings for Donnie. That, and the fact that he, his brother, and Sarah all smoked weed every day.

It was beginning to get out of hand. Sarah was fucking up at her job. She would go in late and leave early. She would rarely come home at night and was getting behind with her part of the rent. I would come home from work some days to find the three of them in her smoke filled bedroom, playing video games, and eating Coney dogs. Donnie would trip on me from time to time about not joining in. Like any other woman, I dug the thug role and his sex was good, but I knew I had to get out of this relationship and back to Kyle.

On Sunday, the four of us hung out at Royals Skateland on Alter Road with the twenty-five and over crowd. No, I wasn't twenty-five yet, but the guy at the door always let me in with Sarah and the twins. I was wearing my tight blue Donna Karen jeans and baby T-shirt. Sarah and David both wore matching FUBU gear, so that everyone knew they were a couple. Donnie and I both thought that was childish but hey that was their thing. We all walked through the crowd of people stopping every two seconds to speak to all the familiar faces until we reached the lockers to lock our shoes up. I was the only one who remembered to bring the quarter to place in the lock so I was the one who held onto the key. The joint was hot and it smelled like sweat and stinky feet but the music was banging. The floor was packed and everybody was hyped up on some old school song the DJ was playing. I had even begun to bob my head to the beat while tying up my laces. I looked up to ask Sarah the name of the song and noticed her and the twins huddled together. So, I stood up to get a better view of what was really going on and saw the three of them each pop a small pill into their mouths.

"Hey! What was that?" I questioned.

"What was what?" Sarah responded.

"Don't play with me Sarah. Did you just take X with the two of them?"

"Alright B. don't trip O.K. It's cool we do this all the time. You want one?"

"Bitch, you know I don't fuck wit none of that shit and you shouldn't either Sarah. Smokin' weed is one thing, but Ecstasy! Oh my God! Girl what is wrong with you? Are you crazy? That shit can really fuck you up."

Pushing past me and putting her arm around David, "O.K. you are going to ruin my high B. We're here to have a good time and I'm not trying to hear this shit right now! You think you know everything Miss Goody two-shoes. You used to be down for whatever, but now that you've got them damn degrees and shit, you think you all dat. Well fuck you! You are still the same trick ass bitch you always been so get away from me wit all that getting high isn't good for you shit."

"Oh now I'm a trick ass bitch, huh. Well Sarah you're right about one thing, I do think I'm all that, you silly bitch, because I am all that and any nigger that was bout something and really cared about you wouldn't let you fuck up your life with drugs."

Obviously high from the X, Sarah positioned herself between the twins and said,

"See B. that's where you wrong, David does care about me and so does Donnie." Then she grabbed Donnie and placed her tongue in his mouth while David smiled and cheered her on loudly.

I was devastated. What the fuck? My roommate and longtime friend had completely lost her mind. She was addicted to Ecstasy and weed, and was fucking two men who were brothers. One of which I thought was my sex partner. Once again I was fooled and heartbroken by someone I deeply and truly loved. Sarah was once my rock, my dog, and my girl through thick and thin. When did she become jealous of me? When did she flip the script?

There was nothing left for me to do at that point, but to leave. I slowly took off my skates and grabbed my shoes from the locker. “Sarah this was really messed up girl, but I still love you. I will have my shit out of the apartment by this weekend. I hope the three of you have a wonderful life together.”

BIANCA

I ran to my car with tears running down my face. I started the engine and backed out of my parking spot only to realize I had nowhere to go. I didn't want to go to the apartment. I didn't have any other friends that I could really call on and I didn't want to call Kyle with another one of my dramatic life scenes after all of this time. So, I did the next best thing and called home.

My mom wasn't home, but I drove to her house anyway and parked in her driveway. I turned the engine off and sat in silence watching the bugs swarm around the streetlights. At that moment I felt my life had become one big cycle of letdowns. What did I do to deserve this? I loved Sarah like a sister. I would have done anything for her. If it had been any other girl I would have let that shit run off my back. I didn't give a damn about Donnie, but Sarah was like a blood relative to me. Where was my mom when I needed her? I opened my glove compartment and pulled out my cell phone and began to scroll through my phonebook to retrieve her cell phone number.

****

It was hard moving back home with my mom after I had been on my own for so long. Three days had gone by since I'd last seen Sarah or my apartment. I went to work on Monday and didn't give her or the ménage trio a second thought. Today was different though. She came across my mind when I stopped into Blockbuster to rent a movie, something she and I used to do together. I was looking through the new releases counting the movies I hadn't seen when I came across the manager's special section and saw *Love Jones* with Larenz Tate. Sarah loved him. She thought he was very sexy. I always thought he was too short to be sexy, but she would always say, "Girl, don't sleep on the shorties."

I smiled. I missed my old friend. I picked up a wide screen copy of the DVD and continued to browse through the rest of the movies. My mom had a date tonight. I'd be solo for the evening, so I'd thought I'd rent two movies, get some popcorn, twizzlers, and a two liter of pepsi, and enjoy the solitude. I made my selections, paid the clerk, and made it home before 6:00 p.m. As I drove up the block I saw neighbors I hadn't seen in months. I honked my horn at the bad kids playing in the street. "Get that damn ball out of the street before I run it and you over!"

"Aw'right Miss Havin, sorry!"

I smiled and waved at Ms. Clark who was walking her dog, and Mr. Peterson who was sitting in his lazy boy looking out of his picture window. The block hadn't changed and it was good seeing all the same people doing the same things.

I took off my clothes, wrapped my hair, put a scarf on and jumped into the shower. Before I started movie night, I put on a facial mask and took out the pants suit I planned on wearing the next day. Then I proceeded to the kitchen to pour myself a tall glass of Pepsi on ice. I'd already placed one of my mom's mugs in the freezer so it would be chilled and frothy for my favorite beverage. I put the popcorn in the microwave and was opening the bag of licorice when the doorbell rang.

"Who could that be?" I mumbled to myself, looking at the clock on the kitchen wall. It was seven o'clock and my mom wasn't home. I started to ignore it and continue on with my private party. "Humph! It isn't for me."

DING DONG DING DONG

"Oh! This fool is tripping! Walking to the door, "Who is it?"

"It's me B. Open the door girl!"

Oh! My god! Looking through the peephole of my mom's steel door, I saw Chauncey's big brown eyes glaring back at me. I slowly opened the door trying to fix the belt on my robe and pull myself together.

"Boy! What are you doing here?"

"I saw your car in the driveway, let me in." He pulled on the handle of the locked screen door. "Are you alone?"

"Yeah. I was getting ready to watch a movie."

Chauncey stepped into the foyer, pulled me into his big arms, and lifted me up into a nice bear hug. "I see you still keeping yourself up nicely."

"What?"

He put me down and pointed to the mirror so that I could see my hair scarf and pale face. "Oh! I was giving myself a facial. Let me go and wash this off."

Running to the bathroom, I turned to him and said, "Come in and have a seat." When I turned to go into the bathroom, I tripped over the hall rug and slightly bumped into the closet door. I was both startled and dazed before I got embarrassed seeing Chauncey point and laugh at me. "Are you that happy to see me?"

Now making it into the bathroom, I turned on the hot water and yelled, "Yeah right! You know better than to just stop by without calling first." I took off my robe, washed my face, and yanked a pair of my mom's dirty jogging pants and a musty T-shirt out of the hamper. Then I snatched my scarf off and brushed my hair back into a ponytail.

When I opened the bathroom door, Chauncey was in the kitchen pouring my popcorn into a bowl. He remembered where those things were as though we'd just broken up yesterday.

"Thanks."

"You're welcome. So what's up? Are you staying here again?"

Carrying my goodies into the den, "Yeah, I had to move out of the apartment. I'll be here for a minute. What's up with you? You looking good."

Now pouring himself a glass of water, "Thank you. I've been doing aw'right for myself. I'm working now and looking for a place to stay."

"That's cool. Where are you working?"

"My boy got me a job over at the Budd plant on Conner."

"Doing what?"

"Janitorial services; I work afternoons."

"Then why aren't you at work now?"

Now sitting close to me, "I took the day off to take care of a few things. Hey, it's a good thing I did or I would not have known you were in the hood again."

Sitting back and adjusting a few pillows, "No I guess you wouldn't have known, huh? I'm only here for a few weeks, tops. Sarah and I had a fight. It's nothing though. It's time I got my own anyway."

"Yeah, I hear dat. My mom has been clowning me lately. I just signed a lease today and got keys to this spot downtown."

"What! You're moving out. Are Kelly and Cicily moving in with you?"

"No, I'm moving alone. I'm paying her child support now and Cicily comes to see me on the weekends."

"You're finally growing up huh!"

"Don't go there B."

"Sorry, you're right. So, where are you on your way to?"

"Are you putting me out?"

"Um, well I guess not, you can stay if you want. I'm just watching a few movies and then going to bed."

Rubbing my leg, "Is your mom coming home soon?"

Avoiding the temptation of his offer, I gently pushed him away and lied, "Yeah, she'll be here any minute now."

"Okay, well maybe I'll stop through on another day."

"Yeah, maybe."

KYLE

"Yeah dad, I'll take care of things on my part. The meeting is next week Wednesday at 9:00 a.m. at the restaurant. I'm going to make the stuffed Cornish hens. They'll love it. Okay, I'll talk to you later. I have to go. Bye."

Tamara sat on the couch waiting for me to get off the phone. "So when are you going to tell your parents?"

"I don't know, maybe when the blood test proves that what you are saying is true."

What do you mean by that? You think I'm making this up? Does my stomach look like I'm making this up Kyle?"

"Look Tamara, I haven't seen you in almost a year. I don't know whose baby you're carrying."

"Kyle it's been nine months, not a year. I was scared. I was unsure about keeping this baby, but I am sure that it's yours."

"You're not sure of anything Tamara and you and I both know it. How many other men have you been with since you left me?

"Fuck you!" Taking off her one of her orange and white DKNY gym shoes and throwing it at me. "You think I need your sorry ass. You think I'd pick you out of all the men I know to be a father for my child."

Now taking off the other shoe to aim. "Huh, do you? Why Kyle? You don't have shit! You're just an okie doke chef trying to be a restaurant owner. But you spend all of your time trying to impress your friends and get your dad's approval. You weren't even man enough to purchase your own house. You lived with your mother until your ol' granny croaked and gave you this one. If I hadn't helped you decorate, this place would still be the dump she left it in. You couldn't even take care of your own cat. Why would I believe you could help me with a child?"

"Okay, now you've gone too far Tamara. You've got to go." I picked up her shoes and carried them over to her.

"Oh, you're putting me out? You've grown some balls since I left. Okay, screw you Kyle. I'll call you when the baby is born and the Friend of the Court will contact you about the child support."

"Okay, do that! I'll call my mother and let her know so that she can set up the joint custody agreement. You're not getting a dime of my money."

"Don't think you're going to get any joint custody because I'll make it so you'll never see this baby."

Grabbing her by the arm, "Tamara, wait! Let's not do things this way. What do you want from me? You left me nine months ago. Now that I'm finally moving on, you come back and spring this on me. If this is my child I want to do my part."

"I want you to be a man and take care of your responsibilities. I need help with this baby, Kyle."

We both stood silently holding hands. The room was so quite you could hear a mouse pass gas. Then my cell phone rang. It was Bill from the restaurant. *"Hey man where are you?"*

"I'm on my way." Focusing back on Tamara, "I have to go." I grabbed my coat and ran out of the door. The dinner crowd was starting to come in at the restaurant and the other head chef needed to leave early today which meant I needed to cover for him this evening. Business was really picking up since I started catering weddings and other functions on the side, which was cool since Tamara had returned with the news she sprang on me. I can't believe I'm going to be a daddy, partly because she's a liar, and because we always used condoms. But if this kid is mine, I am going to take care of it.

BIANCA

Seeing Chauncey again brought back ol' memories of our escapades. I went back and forth with the idea of sleeping with him again. He had left me his new cell phone number that night and my well had run dry. I had not had any dick since Donald. I'm real sick about giving it up to him now.

I walked to the parking lot contemplating my next move. It was Thursday, which used to be my dinner nights with Kyle. I'd thought about surprising him with a visit to the restaurant and talking with him face to face. But that idea faded away as quickly as it had come. I turned on the radio, slid my heels off, and threw them onto the backseat. Working these long hours is starting to wear me out, but I need the money. I want to move back out on my own as quickly as possible. My mom is great, but I love her more when we do not share the same living quarters.

I decided I'd go home and make up my mind on whether I wanted to call Chauncey once I showered and rested for a while. My mom was in the kitchen cooking wearing her usual house dress, an apron, and house shoes. "Hey Ma! I'm home."

"Hey baby. How was work?"

"It was work. What are you cooking?"

"Greens, Mac and cheese, and baked chicken. Maxwell is coming over for dinner. We're going to eat and play Chinese checkers. He always lets me win when I feed him a good meal first."

"Sounds like tons of fun, Ma. Don't hurt him."

"What you got up for this evening?"

"I don't know yet."

"You got some phone messages while you were at work. I left them over there on the table. One is from a Donald. He said it was urgent that you call him as soon as you got in."

"Donald? What does he want?" Grabbing my messages off the writing pad on the table, I flipped through and glanced at my mom's scribbled writing.

"I don't know, he didn't say. Maybe you should call him and find out."

"Thanks Ma. I'm going to take a shower and eat, then I'll call everybody back." I ran upstairs and took off my skirt and stockings. Then, I laid across my bed and closed my eyes. I had only intended on resting for a few minutes, but when my mom smacked my butt and gave me the phone, the clock said an hour had gone by.

"It's that Donald guy again. He says its important. It's about Sarah."

Rolling over, I thought this had better be important. Taking the phone from my mom,

"Hello."

"Yeah B., it's me Donald. Look, don't hang up aw'right. Listen, Sarah is in the hospital and it doesn't look good. She's had a stroke. They're saying she might not make it."

"What? What happened? Where is she? What hospital?"

"Henry Ford on the Boulevard. My brother and her mother are there with her now. I just thought I'd call to let you know."

"Thanks Donald. I appreciate it."

Hanging up, I gave my mom the phone and got dressed. I had to go see my friend. I needed to know that she was okay.

BIANCA

My mom drove me to the hospital. She'd cancelled her checker game and sent Max, her date, home with his plate of food. He was cool. He offered his support to both my mom and me and told her to call him later. I was a wreck. I started thinking that this could have all been prevented had I stayed with her.

My mom let me out at the front door while she went to park the car. I ran in, got a visitor's pass, and hurried to her floor. When I got to her room, her mom, and a few of her family members were standing around waiting on the doctor to come out. When her mom saw me she began walking towards me ranting and raving, "How dare you show up here, you tramp! You got my baby mixed up in all this shit and then you left her alone to pay all those bills by herself. She was stressed out and that's why she's here now. How dare you come here?" I was in shock and completely thrown off by her accusations. Her husband and a few other people were holding her back. I started to back away, "Ms. Pickett what are you talking about? Sarah was using drugs and I didn't leaveher without paying my half of the bills. I don't know what's going here, but..."

Before I could finish my plea, she broke loose, ran up on me, and slapped me across the face three times before anyone could grab her again.

"You liar! My daughter has never used a drug a day in her life. You get out of here right now or I'll kill you."

Just then the elevator doors opened up again and my mom stepped out. "What's going on? What's all the commotion?" Helping me up off the floor, "Bianca what happened?"

"I'm okay mom, let's go. I'll just call back later to check on her."

"Why? Why is that woman yelling at you like that?"

Then, turning to address Sarah's mom, "If you come near my daughter again bitch, you'll have me to deal with!"

Now pulling my mom by the arm into the elevator doors, "It's cool mommy, I'm okay, come on."

BIANCA

I laid in bed the next morning thinking about the way things had turned out last night. I really wanted to see Sarah and tell her how much I missed and loved her. We were best friends and I should not have let anything come between us.

I rolled over to pick up the remote so that I could watch the morning news for the weather forecast. I changed the channel and tuned in to Fox 2. I was a little upset that Rhonda Walker had left the show, but the new girl was aw'right. I sat up in the bed to stretch my muscles, then I yawned.

"Another day of paper chasing."

I got up and went to the closet to pick out an outfit to wear to work. I smelled the bacon cooking in the kitchen and assumed my mom was already awake. "Ma cook me some, too!" I yelled down from the top of the stairs. That was one of the perks in moving back home.

I got dressed in racetrack time and hurried down to the kitchen to pack myself a lunch. I'd saved $30 a week by taking sandwiches from home instead of eating take out. My mom had left my breakfast of scrambled eggs, bacon, and toast covered on top of the stove, so I snatched it up on my way out of the door. I planned on getting to work at least a half an hour earlier today so that I could leave a half an hour earlier this afternoon. I wanted to stop by the hospital and possibly see Sarah before the rest of her family members would get there. Lord knows I didn't want to get into another altercation with her mom.

When I arrived at my desk, a handsome delivery guy who held a beautiful bouquet of yellow roses greeted me.

"Are you Ms. B. Havin?"

"Humph, not lately."

He stared at me blankly, "What?"

"Nothing. Are these for me?"

"Yes, um are you Ms. Bianca Havin?"

"Yes, I'm sorry for the joke. You obviously didn't get it."

Ignoring me, "The guy said to make sure I give these directly to you."

Taking the load off his hands. "Thanks, who are they from?"

"A Mr. Sinclair, ma'am."

"Ooh, from Kyle." I smelled the flowers and pulled the small vanilla envelop out of the box. It read, "Bianca I miss you and would love to hear from you again. Please call me. Love, Kyle."

I smiled, it had been two weeks since we'd spoken to each other. A lot had changed for me in the last fourteen days. I needed a good ear to listen to my whining. I took off my coat and placed the flowers on my desk. I picked up the receiver to the phone and dialed his number.

"Hello"

"Oh, I'm sorry I must have dialed the wrong number. I'll try again."

The woman chuckled a little, "Yeah O.K."

I hung up and slowly redialed. Again, a woman answered, "Hello."

I paused, "Um, hello is Kyle there?"

"No he isn't, may I ask who's calling?"

"This is Bianca. Who is this?"

"This is Tamara, Kyle's fiancee. He's not in at the moment Bianca, but I will tell him you called. Is there a message?"

What fiancee? "No, I don't want to leave a message. I'll try his cell phone. Bye."

Hanging up, I looked at the phone and then around the office. People were still walking around and getting settled in, but I felt like time was standing still. It was like I was in the Twilight Zone. "When did Kyle get engaged and who the hell is Tamara?"

I got up and walked to the coffee machine in the staff lounge to collect my thoughts. As I poured the hot beverage into the small Styrofoam cup I began talking to myself aloud again, "She's the ex-girlfriend! When did she come back? Shit! Why did she come back? What is Kyle doing?" It was obvious that I was confused as hell. I walked back to my desk mumbling, half hearing, and half speaking to my co-workers who were greeting me. When I got back to my desk, Sherry and a few other women were standing around admiring my beautiful bouquet of flowers. "Wow! Girl these are nice. Who sent them?"

Moving past them and sitting down, "Huh?"

"Girl who sent you these gorgeous flowers? I'm jealous. They smell so good!"

Snapping out of it, I responded, "Oh, just a friend."

KYLE

"Eh, why were you answering my phone? I asked you not to do that."

"Oh stop trippin'. It was just some chick. I think she said her name was Beyonce' or something like that."

"Bianca?"

"Yeah, I guess." Laughing, "I told her I was your fiancee'. I don't think she'll be calling you again."

"I could kill you! Why would you tell her something like that? Are you crazy?"

"No I'm not crazy? Are you?"

"Yes, crazy for letting you back in my house. Look, I said you could stay here until the painters finished your apartment, but I think it's time for you to go now. You need to call them, go home, and open up some windows or something. I can give you a couple of fans."

"Oh now you're trying to put me out. I'm pregnant with your baby and I can't stand those paint fumes. I'm not going anywhere."

Grabbing her coat and purse, and walking towards the door, "Yes you are. Get the hell out of here right now."

"You can't do this to me Kyle! I don't have anywhere else to go."

"Go to a hotel, call me and I'll split the bill with you." Now picking up her suitcase and sitting it outside of the door, "Hell, I'll pay the whole bill, but you cannot stay here."

"Okay, I'm sorry. Don't put me out. I'll call her back and apologize. I don't want to leave. I don't want to be alone."

"No Tamara. Get out!"

Now stomping past me and taking her coat out of my hands, "You'll be sorry!"

Closing the door behind her. "I'm already sorry. Sorry I ever fooled around with you."

I walked over to the couch and sat for a moment. "Damn, what am I going to say to Bianca now?" I closed my eyes, rubbed my temples, and enjoyed the peace and quiet. That is until I heard the alarm on my truck sounding. "This girl!" I ran to the window and peeped out of the blinds. Tamara was standing next to my car holding up a tire wrench in one hand and the middle finger on her other hand, swearing at me. She had broken out my windshield and was threatening to hit the driver's side window if I didn't let her back into the house. I closed the blinds and went into the back of the house where I couldn't hear her ranting and raving. I thought maybe after she's broken out all of the windows she'd get tired and leave me the hell alone. I was right. After ten more minutes, she was gone.

BIANCA

I was spending another night alone at my mom's house wondering what had happen to all of my men. Specifically, what happened with my Kyle? Should I call him? Should I wait for him to call me? I didn't know how to handle this news about his getting married. I didn't have Sarah to ask for advice and my mom was entertaining Max.

Their giggling was beginning to annoy me. I thought about just getting into my car and going for a drive, but changed my mind and turned on the television instead. However after about twenty minutes into a rerun of the Jamie Fox Show, my mom's giggling turned into moaning. Then, I heard Max yelling out "Oh yeah baby, I loved this pussy!"

My stomach turned over twelve times. I turned up the volume, but it seemed like the louder the television got, the louder they got. I thought this is definitely one of the downfalls of moving back home with mom.

I turned off the television, grabbed my brown leather jacket and purse, and decided to sit outside on the porch until I decided where I was going to go. The cool wind whipped up around me and quickly brought tears to my eyes. "Shit, I need to sit in the car." I pushed the alarm button and ran to get inside. Once I shut the door, I stuck the key in the ignition. I rubbed my hands together and began searching for my CD case on the back seat when I heard a vibrating noise coming from the front of the car. "Oh please don't tell me something is rattling on this mutherfucker." I turned the radio off and sat quietly for a moment hoping the rattling would stop. Then I heard it again, "Damn what is that?" I picked my purse up off the floor, and leaned in closer to the dashboard. Then I heard it again, only this time my purse began shaking in my hand. It was my cell phone vibrating. My heart skipped a beat and I smiled. I wiped the tears from my eyes, reached inside, pulled it out, and pushed the button to speak to the one person I knew I could always count on. "Hello stranger!" Trying to sound chipper. "I haven't heard from you in a while. Where've you been?"

"No, the question is where've you been? I haven't heard from you in two weeks. I need to see you are you free tomorrow?"

"I'm free tonight! I need to see you, too. Can you come over and help me pack up a few of my things. I need a place to stay for a few days."

"Yeah baby, what's up? Are you and Sarah fighting? Are you O.K.?"

"I'll tell you everything once you get here."

Breaking into a loud cry, my voice began to crack, "I just really need somewhere I can go and think about everything that's been going on in my life."

There was silence on the other end of the phone, then he spoke, "I knew it was time for me to call you. I'll come and get you? Wherever you are I can be there in five minutes."

"I'm at home. I mean at my mother's house. Do you remember the address? My car is parked in the driveway. I'll sit here until you come. Thanks Kyle. Thanks a lot for everything. I know I've been a pain in the ass to you and you've been a good friend to me from the beginning. I can always count on you and I appreciate that. I need to explain a lot of things to you and apologize for my behavior. I want you to know that those other guys meant nothing to me. It took me a while to understand that, but now everything is finally clear. I love you Kyle and I'm ready for us to go to that next level with each other. That is if you'll still have me?"

"Bianca you know that I still want to be with you. How can you ask me something like that? Even after all this time, my heart still belongs to you. I need you to always remember that. Something has come up and there are some things we'll need to discuss and work out before we decide to commit to one another. I'm on my way. We'll talk baby, we'll talk."

"O.K. Thanks again Kyle." Hanging up the phone, I grabbed a McDonald's napkin from the glove compartment and wiped my face dry. I turned the radio up. I felt better after talking to Kyle and I wanted to hear something upbeat. Nothing good was on the radio, so I grabbed my CD case from the floor and flipped through the various diskettes. I decided to listen to Mary J. Blige's, "Share My World." I was so happy that I'd finally told Kyle how I felt about him. I was a little puzzled about the way he took that information though. He didn't seem excited or surprised to hear me say those three beautiful words. I couldn't help but to feel something was wrong. Was he really engaged to Tamara? Why did she answer his telephone? Something was going on with Kyle and I felt it. What did he have to talk about with me? What was so serious that we had to discuss it before we could be together? Was he still mad at me for dating other guys? Yeah, that had to be it. If he wanted to know if I could be faithful to him, he had nothing to worry about.

BIANCA

When Kyle pulled up behind my car there were twenty butterflies in my stomach. My mom's company had left. So she'd come out to the car with a glass of lemonade and inquired as to why I was out there. She didn't know how emotional I had been. She hugged me and was very surprised. I told her that I was going to leave my car at her house for a little while and that I'd be staying with Kyle for a few days if she needed to get in touch with me. I asked her not to tell anyone where I was going to be. She understood and said, "Sometimes you need to get away baby, even if it's just for a day or two. It helps you to collect your thoughts. Have fun. Your secret is safe with me. When you're ready to come back home, I'll be here."

Sometimes I really loved talking to my mom. I opened the door and hugged Kyle as tight as I could. I had really missed him. We held each other and didn't say a word for what seemed to be ten minutes. When we pulled apart from each other, he noticed my mom standing in doorway. He yelled out, "How are you Ms. Havin? It's good to see you again."

She responded, "Same here Kyle. You take care of my baby, I'll see you guys later."

I locked the doors on my car and Kyle escorted me to his. When he got in on his side I leaned over and hugged him again. "Oh! Baby it is so good to see you again. I have truly missed you. You are not going to believe all of the things that have been going on in my life. But first tell me what's been going on in your life. Who is Tamara and why is she claiming to be your fiancee?"

Cutting me off, Kyle pulled back and said, "Bianca, you are not going to believe what has been going on in my life. I don't mean to cut you off and I know that you are going through some things right now, but I need you to just listen to me right now. You and I really need to talk. I have gotten myself into something and I don't know how I'm going to get out of it."

Taken off guard, I positioned myself to look Kyle directly in the eyes. "O.K. Boo, what's up? If I can help you, I will. What's wrong?"

Backing out of my mom's driveway, he turned the volume on the radio down, and then held my hand. When I saw you out with that guy at the comedy club, Bianca, I was hurt. I knew that you were still dating other guys and I was trying to deal with that, but seeing you with him really hurt. I love you girl, more than any other woman that I've ever been with and I need you to remember that when I say what I'm about to say."

"Kyle, I love you, too. I didn't mean for you to

see me with Donnie and I never meant to hurt you in any way. I tried calling you that night to tell you that I was ready to be with you, but you didn't answer your phone. I only went out with Sarah and those guys to pass the time until I could talk to you. It hurt me that you were with another woman, too. You told me that you would wait for me and when I saw you with her, I thought that you'd betrayed me."

"I know you did. I wanted to call you afterwards, but I felt it was time to let you go. You didn't want what I wanted and my friends were telling me I was a fool for waiting for you. I let them and that girl get in my head, and I messed up baby. I'm sorry."

"Sorry for what? Kyle what is it that you have to tell me?"

"I have a child. Tamara, my ex-girlfriend, she says we have a child. I mean she's pregnant. She says the baby is mine and I just don't know what I'm going to do. I'm willing to take care of my responsibilities, but I do not want to be bothered with her ass for the rest of my life Bianca."

Once again my heart skipped a beat. I had never heard Kyle curse before. Words like that usually came from my potty mouth. It felt strange. It was like I was hearing a broken record being played over and over. Chauncey had said those same words to me seven years ago in high school. My boyfriend is going to be someone else's baby's daddy again. Why me? I turned to look out of the window on my side of the car. I was disgusted and hurt all over again. When I tried to speak, the lump in my throat prevented the sound from escaping, and the tears began to roll down my face again. I took a deep breath, wiped my cheek with the back of my hand, and then I spoke, "Kyle pull the car over and let me out right here."

"Bianca no! I'm not letting you out in the middle of the street. I'm taking you home with me so we can work this out together. You said that you were in love and ready to be with me. I'm not letting you go now. I need you. Don't run out on me again."

I grew angry and repeated myself in a louder tone, "Kyle pull this mutherfucker over and let me out right now!"

In an even louder tone, he responded, "NO! Bianca you are stuck with me. You said you wanted to be with me and now you are. Fuck that I'm not letting you go again. This shit is messed up, but it's done now. Besides, I don't even know if the baby is mine for sure."

"What do you mean you don't know if it's yours? You slept with her without a condom Kyle. What the fuck is wrong with you men? If you don't trust her enough to believe that she's telling the truth about having your baby, why would you trust her enough to have sex with her with a raw ass dick? How do you trust that she's telling the truth about not having AIDS or any other STD, but you don't have trust in her to believe she's carrying your seed?"

"Bianca I did use a condom with her. She's saying that it must have come off or something or that it had a hole in it? That's why I don't trust her. We'd both been drinking the night before she left me and she was insisting on having sex. She even put the condom on me and took it off. I think it was a set up honestly. I think she knew she was pregnant before that night and now she wants to pin it on me. I really think she's fucking with me B. and that's why I need you to be patient and just stay with me until I work this shit out. Please! I'm always here for you Bianca, I need you to be here for me now."

With that last statement I knew I couldn't do anything but stand by his side. Kyle had never used such profanity in all the days that I've known him. He was right, too. Whenever I've needed him in the past he's always been there for me. For some reason I felt I was being tested, but I was determined to pass. "Kyle this baby better not be yours. I'm going to ride this out with you, but if you're lying to me I am going to fuck you up. Do you understand me?"

"Yeah I hear you."

"Take me home."

"Do you want to talk about what's going on with you too?"

"Maybe tomorrow. I have a huge headache right now."

KYLE

"I've been kissing Bianca's butt for the last few days now, dawg. But it's cool. I'm just happy she's back in my life. Once I do this dinner party for the mayor on Wednesday night and close some deals with my investors, I can open up my restaurant and propose to my Boo!"

"Wait a minute, you're thinking about marrying this broad? You really believe she's the one? You've only known her a few months."

"This is the one. She does it for me man."

"Does she know?"

"Naw, I'm going to surprise her. My mom is going to help me pick out a ring this weekend."

"What are you going to do about Tamara and the baby?"

"Oh, I got something planned for her. My dad has hired a P.I. He's been following her and checking up on things for us. My mom has already drawn up some custody and support papers. If things go as planned, everything should be cool."

"So what's up with this dinner? You Mr. Big Time now, cooking for Kwame and all."

"Yeah, my dad hooked things up with the Mayor's people and it's going down the day after tomorrow. A few photographers, a reporter from Fox 2 and some writers from a couple of the local newspapers will be there to cover the story. I will be in rare form. I'm cooking my stuffed Cornish hens, macaroni and cheese, greens, and I used my grandma's recipe for homemade rolls. For dessert I'm serving an apple cake and French vanilla ice cream with a pinch of cinnamon sprinkled on top."

"Yeah, that ought to get them. Shit, I'm getting hungry listening to you. Man, let me go get something to eat. I'll holler at you later."

"Yeah, peace."

Hanging up my cordless phone, I got out of bed and placed it on the charger. This making up sex had me spent. I was tired! I turned off my alarm clock so that I could sleep a little late today, but I didn't know it was already 11:00 a.m. Bianca must have left quietly this morning. I didn't hear her get in the shower. I need to get in the bathroom and get dressed so I can make my 1:00 appointment with Paul and Clarence, two of my dad's closest friends. They were going to back me with half of the money I need to buy the building downtown. I saved my half of the $250,000 through working overtime, covering shifts for the other chefs and catering private events with the exception of the $10,000 I was going to make on Wednesday. This dinner would be the last hustle I needed to put me at $125,000. Once I closed on the building, I could use it as collateral when I went to the bank to apply for the small business loan I needed to open up SINCLAIR'S.

Looking at myself in the mirror, I smiled as the foam of toothpaste dripped down into my beard. "Yeah, this is going to be tight. I'll have my business and a beautiful woman by my side. Life is good!"

I hopped into the shower, got dressed, and made myself some lunch before heading out. I thought about calling B. before I left, but decided to wait until after the meeting so I could share the good news with her.

Paul and Clarence were waiting patiently for me at the bar in the restaurant. I had a hard time finding a parking spot downtown at this time of day. It was during the lunchtime rush. I opted to give my truck to the valet attendant after ten minutes of circling the block.

Paul stood up and shook my hand when I approached the two gentlemen. Clarence nodded and held up his drink.

"Paul. Clarence. Good seeing you again. How's it going?"

"Good. Things are well Kyle. How are you?"

"Good Paul. Thanks for asking. So Clarence, what's up guy? How've you been?"

"Good thanks."

"Well gentlemen, shall we get down to business?"

"Yeah I see you've come prepared. Let's take a look at your business plan over a few drinks.

What'll you have?"

Handing him the vanilla folder and turning to the bartender, "A coke please." Then addressing Clarence,

"Here's your copy."

"I won't be needing this Kyle. I spoke with your father and I am fully aware of your plans."

"Are you sure you don't want to take a look?"

"I'm positive. In fact, I've already written out the check. I've asked my lawyer, your mom, to write up the contract for the repayment of this loan. You should receive it by messenger tomorrow. Look over it, if you agree with it, sign it and return it to her."

"That's it. Is it that easy Clarence?"

"No, I just really trust you and your dad. I know you guys are good for it."

"Thanks man. Thanks. You won't regret this." Now turning to Paul, "Well what do you think?"

"Everything looks good so far. Hell, I'd be an ass now if I said no. Clarence has put on the pressure. How about I read over the rest of this tonight and have my lawyer bring over the papers tomorrow."

"Aw wow! Aw man, guys this is great! You two have just made my day."

"Well you haven't read through our terms yet. Don't get too excited." Clarence cautioned before taking another sip of his drink.

"Yeah, you're right. But I'm too happy not to get excited. This has been my dream for a long time now. I'm willing to do whatever to make this come true," shaking their hands. "Thanks guys, really, thank you."

Now smiling, Paul extended his hand to mine. "You're welcome, son, you're welcome. Are you leaving?"

"Yeah, I got a few more errands to run for the big dinner party I'm catering for Mayor Kilpatrick on Wednesday."

Before finishing his drink, Clarence spoke, "Oh yeah, your dad was telling us about that. Congratulations and good luck."

"Thanks man. I'll be seeing you guys real soon."

I walked out of the restaurant feeling higher than a kite. I was on cloud nine. I took a few deep breaths and reached inside my pants pocket for the valet ticket. The attendant looked at me strangely and asked, "Are you alright?" Smiling and handing him the ticket, "Yeah man, I'm just fine. Hah Hah, I'm doing great!"

KYLE

"Eh, baby! Baby, wake up."

Rolling over slowly, "Why? What time is it?"

Pulling the covers back, "It's 6:30, wake up. You'll be late for work. Here, I brought some juice and a bagel. Get up!"

"No, I don't want to."

"Yeah, I know. We may have over done it with the celebrating last night, huh?"

"Yeah, just a little. But it doesn't look like it's bothering you any."

"Naw, baby it's not. I'm too hyped to be tired. The contracts are coming today and I need to get prepared for tomorrow."

"I think I'm going to call in and just work from home today."

"That's cool, I'll enjoy your company. You can stay here while I run out to do some last minute things."

"Oh so now you want to use me."

"Never that. I really do need you to be here to get those papers."

"O.K. I can do that for you Boo. Let me get up and brush my teeth. I can smell my own breath and it isn't nice."

"I know. I'm glad you noticed."

Hitting me with her pillow, "Hah hah, you weren't complaining about my breath last night."

Chasing her into the bathroom, "You weren't complaining much last night either. All I heard was, oh Kyle don't stop baby, and this pussy is yours baby."

Closing the door in my face, "Yeah right, I don't even use that word."

Yelling through the door, "Well you did last night and if you open this door I'll make you say it again this morning."

"Is that a challenge?"

"Naw baby that's a promise. "Opening the door, she stood butt naked, "Bring it."

Pulling her in close to me and kissing her passionately, "You know I love you don't you?"

"Yes and I love you."

"Hmm, say it again."

"I love you."

Lifting her up into my arms, I carried her over to the bed, slowly spread her legs open, and whispered, "Say it again."

Holding my head between her thighs, she fell back onto the pillows and moaned, "Kyle baby, I love you."

"Tell me this pussy is mine."

"This pussy is all yours."

BIANCA

Kyle drove me to my old apartment and I collected all of my suits, skirts, and shoes and put them in my suitcases. I went into my bathroom and got the rest of my toiletries and took my scarf out of the bathroom drawer. The whole apartment was dark and quiet with the exception of the lights I'd turned on in my bedroom and in the restroom. Kyle sat on the couch and watched me in silence as I walked through the living room mumbling about Sarah being nasty. He could tell I was really pissed off with her. When I finally finished packing I had two suitcases and an overnight bag full of shoes and accessories. I stood in front of him and looked around the apartment as if to take one last inventory of everything.

Finally he spoke, "Uh baby is that everything?"

"Yes, I think I'm done. I'm moving out of here."

"Do you want me to take these to the car?"

"Yeah, you grab those two and I'll get this bag."

I turned off the lights, followed Kyle out of the door, and locked it behind me. I thought to myself, "I'm going to miss this place. I had some good times here." When I left that parking lot with Kyle that night I closed that chapter of my life for good. I sent Sarah my key and parking pass in the mail. I never spoke to her again after that. I never attempted to call or go to the hospital again. I never regretted that move either.

My mom said that Sarah had called her house a few times and wanted to know how I was doing, but she would always give her the same dry answer. "Oh Bianca is doing fine, honey. She's doing real well. I'll tell her you asked about her." Nothing more and nothing less. She said Sarah didn't sound healthy anymore and that she'd heard that she had lost a lot of weight. I didn't question it any further and I never told my mom exactly what had happened that night or why I decided to move out. She never asked. I believed my mom knew what was going with my ex-best friend.

I got an apartment in Dearborn, which was closer to my job. It had two bedrooms, a living room, dining room, and one and a half bathrooms. It also had an extended balcony so that I could have a perfect view of just about everything on my side of the building. Kyle had helped me furnish it, since my move was so sudden. He hired his mother's interior decorator to come in and plush my new crib out. I loved it! But I hated not being closer to him. With everything going on with Tamara, her baby drama, and his job, we barely got to see each other.

We still had our Thursday night dinner dates at

the restaurant, and we started going to church together on Sundays, but getting together between those days was hard.

My company had begun laying people off due to downsizing and so the grind was on for me. I had to prove that I was an asset to the company as not to lose my job. I would go in early and stay late many nights just to keep up with all of my accounts. There were a lot of people on edge. The stress factor around my office was at its peak high. You could feel the tension in the air. There were even some supervisors and executives who were being pink slipped at the drop of a dime. It felt like I was working for the post office and at any minute someone was going to flip and kill us all.

At times, I would come in from work and simply pass out on the couch with my clothes still on. I knew that I had to find something else soon. My body and mind couldn't take that kind of pressure. I began looking in the newspaper for new positions on my lunch hour and I'd even put my resume on the Internet.

On Tuesday, after checking my e-mail one more time for new job offers, I decided to call it a day and go home early. I packed up belongings, put my date book in my bag, and grabbed my sweater. I walked to the elevator and pushed the circular down button and began to pace as I waited. When the doors opened, I jumped at the screeching sound of someone screaming out my name.

"Oh! My god Bianca Havin! Is that you girl?"

I looked up and around to see if anyone else thought the building was burning down. The voice was familiar, but the face was a little distorted. It looked liked my old high school girlfriend, Cynthia, but her frame was a lot smaller, and her hair was short. The Cynthia I once knew in high school was a big girl and her hair was long and thick. She was the only person I knew who had to get her hair permed exactly every six weeks. She was a lot prettier than this skinny chicken head little woman who was standing in front of me.

"Cynt, girl is that you? How long has it been? How've you been?"

Cynthia opened her arms up and hugged me real tight. "Girl I have been trying to get in contact with you. My life has been one big world wind of trouble. I've been so stressed out about everything."

When the doors closed on the elevator I stepped back to look her more closely in the face, then reached over and pushed the first floor button. "Girl, I know what you mean. This job is a trip isn't it? What do you do here? Have there been many layoffs on your floor? Girl you didn't get a pink slip did you?"

She smiled, "Naw girl, they haven't let me go yet! Lord knows I would love to sit on my ass and collect an unemployment check. I'm an administrative assistant in the advertising department on the sixth floor. What do you do?"

"I'm an accountant here. So what's been up

with you?"

"Girl there isn't enough time in the day to begin telling you all of the stuff that's been going on with me. Where are you going? You want to go to a happy hour with me to get a few drinks?"

I thought about everything I had planned for the evening, which was nothing. Kyle was working. I had some files that I needed to look through, but those can wait another day or so. I could use a drink with all of the things that were going on in my own life. I wasn't that enthusiastic about hearing Cynthia's problems, but what the hell, maybe her situation would make me forget about my own damn problems.

"Sure, girl I'll hang with you. Where are we going?"

"There's this club on Six mile off of the Southfield freeway called The Comfort Zone. They have live jazz and poetry readings on Tuesdays. My coworkers have all been talking about it. They say it's real nice. We could check that out if you're into that kind of stuff."

"Yeah, that's cool. I like jazz. It would be like that movie Love Jones with Nia Long and Lorenz Tate, huh?"

"I guess so! Let's pop our fingers like the audience did in that flick, too!"

"Girl, I see you're still crazy! Hey should I go home and change or is this outfit O.K. to wear there?"

"Well, I heard it was a happy hour event, so I assume we can wear what we have on. Those slacks look good on you girl, you still have that perfect size ten figure."

"Thanks, Cynt'." Then lying, I said, "Girl you don't look that bad yourself. You still have that pretty smile."

When the doors opened we both walked through the lobby and discussed some old times.

Cynthia was a real good friend to me in high school. I couldn't figure out why we didn't keep in touch. We met while trying out for the varsity cheerleading team during our junior year. When neither one of us made the squad, she slept with the captain of the basketball team and I the captain of the football team just to get back at the sluts who said we weren't varsity material. We called ourselves the Cutie Pies and were envied by the girls, and quite popular with all of the guys. Cynthia's mom and dad had bought her a small used burgundy Dodge Shadow, so she and I would often skip our fifth and sixth hour classes and go to the mall or get breakfast together during our first and second hour classes. We shared each others clothes and even double dated a few times.

I followed her to the bar and reminisced about all of the good times we shared. That was the kind of friendship I regretted not holding onto. Cynthia was a good, kind-hearted person. I was glad that I had bumped into her that day. I started to feel good all over again and was happy that I'd accepted her offer to hang out. However, I was a little concerned about what was going on in her life now that had made her go from diva to scallywag in the few years we'd been apart. I'd hoped it was nothing to serious, but I decided that whatever it was I was going to attempt to be the friend I was to her in high school and help her out if I could.

When we got to the club, we both paid the valet to park our cars. We walked in arm and arm laughing and giggling like teenage girls all over again. Once on the inside I noticed a lot of faces from the job, so I smiled and nodded appropriately. We sat at one of the bar stool tables near the bar in the non-smoking section and Cynt' motioned to the waitress to come over to us.

"What are you drinking Bianca, the first round is on me?"

"I'll have a long island."

Facing the waitress, "We'll have two long islands please."

"This is a nice place Cynt'. Thanks for inviting me."

"You're welcome. Thanks for coming with me. It's been hard finding a good friend to come out with lately. People are so funny nowadays you don't know who's really a friend or a foe. I like that even though you and I haven't spoken in all this time that we can still talk and have fun together."

"I hear that. My best friend and I just got into it big and I haven't spoken to her for a few weeks now. I realized she wasn't that good of a friend to me after all."

"What'd she do, sleep with your man?"

"How'd you know? Actually he wasn't my man he was a friend."

"That's why I don't have any friends B. None of my girls ever slept with my man, but with all this stuff you see on Jenny Jones, Maury, and that Jerry Springer I wouldn't put it past a hoe. Shit, at least your man slept with another woman."

"Yeah that's true, I think I would have felt a lot worse if I was clipped by another man."

The waitress returned with our drinks and Cynthia paid her and gave her a nice tip. Then after taking a sip from her straw, she took a deep breath and said, "Yeah, I can tell you how bad it is losing your man to another man. It's the worst kind of pain ever."

"What? Girl you have got to be playing with me. Your man left you for another man?"

"Yeah, girl. I'm still getting over that shit today. It's been almost two years now and I still get a little down about it."

"Do you want to talk about it?"

"What's to say? I thought I met a real nice guy and he turned out to be a gay guy. End of story!"

Seeing the pain in her eyes, I put my drink down and stood up to hug her. "Girl, FUCK EM'!"

Smiling and half way laughing, "Yeah FUCK EM'! The bastard! What kind of role model will he be for our son?"

Cutting her off, I jumped in, "Your son! Girl you and this guy have a child together? You have got to tell me this story. How did you fuck a gay ass dude and not know?"

"Baby, it wasn't like I knew he was gay. I'm not that stupid! Naw, he was doing that shit on the down low tip. Yeah, I met him at a club one night and we hit it off pretty well. He had good conversation, nice clothes, a good job; he came from a good family, yadda yadda yadda.

We'd been dating for almost three months before he'd even attempted to sleep with me. Then one day while we were hanging out around my crib, he kissed me. That turned in to oral sex, which turned into real sex. It was good, too. His body was tight, he moved real slowly, his penis was a good fit, and he even said some of that freaky shit in my ear. It wasn't until I got pregnant and he proposed marriage that I started getting bugs dropped in my ear that he was playing on the other side of the fence. This guy who goes to my church and is blatantly gay started pulling me to the side telling me that he and my man were lovers, or should I say had been intimate with each other."

"You didn't believe him?"

"Well, at first I didn't. Shit, you know if a bitch will lie to you about sleeping with your man a gay ass man will too."

"So what did you do?"

"I asked Tim about it one night after we'd just made love and were laying in the bed. He denied everything. He got irate and told me I was stupid for believing some fag at my church. He said everyone in my church was a hypocrite and that I needed to stop going there altogether. When I asked him why he was getting so upset, he said that I should never question a man's sexuality like that."

"What? So how did it all come out?"

"A few weeks had gone by and I just let it all go. I didn't mention it anymore, but I started watching his ass real close. I started noticing everything about his ass. I wrote down when he went to work, what time he got off, how long it took him to get home. Girl, I even paid one of my girlfriends to follow him with me on the weekends in her car. You know when you start looking for shit you find it."

"So, you saw him with another guy? What were they doing?"

Cynthia took another sip of her alcoholic beverage, wiped a small tear from her face, smirked and finished her story, "Well, I didn't see all of that, but we did end up at the guy from my church's house. When he opened the door, he smiled at Tim like he'd just won the lottery, stepped aside and let him in. I told my girl to park the car and we sat there for about five minutes before I decided to go and knock on the door. When ol' boy asked who it was, I said Cynt'. He opened the door butt ass naked, and pointed in the direction of his living room where Tim was sitting on the couch with his pants down around his ankles, looking like Boo Boo the Fool."

At this point I could tell she was still in pain so I stopped interrogating her and tried to be supportive. "Oh my goodness! Girl are you O.K.?

Damn! You need a hug. Let me order you another drink. This down low shit out here is for real, huh? I've read some of those E. Lynn Harris books, but I didn't think I'd ever really come across anyone who was doing that shit for real."

"Yeah, I didn't think so either. I called off the wedding, and almost lost my baby behind that shit. I got so depressed. I stopped eating. I wouldn't go out and I stopped taking care of myself all together. Once my baby was born, I was thirty pounds lighter than I was before the pregnancy. Girl you know I was stacked in high school. Look at me now. "

"I didn't want to say anything, but girl you'll be aw'right! Does Tim still come around?"

"Yeah, he and I came to an agreement on visitation, but I haven't even been trying to see anybody else since that shit. This pussy has been on lock for two years. I was nervous as hell when they did that AIDS test in the hospital."

Laughing out loud, "I guess so. That would have me terrified, too. You know that bitch ass Chauncey I use to date gave me some shit not too long ago."

"What! You and that fine ass Chauncey were still seeing each other. You knew he wasn't about nothing in school when he fucked that other girl. Why'd you still waste your time with that mutherfucker?"

Holding up my glass to give her a light toast, I started smiling, "Because I didn't have you around then to tell me to leave his ass alone."

Holding up her glass to mine, "Well here I am baby and I'm going to tell you the truth and nothing but the truth on all this crazy shit out here!"

"To good friends!"

"Salute!"

BIANCA

Over the next few days Cynthia and I began hanging tight. It helped me get through the rough stags Kyle and I were beginning to have with him being so busy with his job, Tamara, and his side-catering gig. He and his dad were trying to open up the soul food restaurant, which included the catering service and a dining hall. Tamara was in her last month, so she was quite the pain in the ass. Kyle hired a midwife to check on her from time to time, but that wasn't enough. I had been through all of the same drama with Chauncey and his baby's momma six years ago. I was still very much in love with Kyle, but I felt things were beginning to change. Instead of going to dinner with him every Thursday, Kyle went to Lamaze classes with Tamara.

So, Cynthia and I would go shopping or to the spa for massages and pedicures. I felt our rekindled friendship was helping Cynt' get through her depression as well. She began writing poems to express her feelings and she read them out loud at the Happy Hour on Tuesdays. We also signed up for ballroom and hustle lessons at the community center near my apartment. There weren't that many single men there so we had to be each other's partner often. It was cool though, we got to laugh at each other and just have fun.

With the exception of our fine ass dance instructor, I think Cynthia was beginning to give up on men. I would see her smiling at him and flirting here and there, but nothing to serious. I talked her into going to my hairdresser at the time to get one of those stylish Halle Berry haircuts. Her hair was broken off quite a bit from all of the stress she was going through, but my girl was able to hook her up. Still, she did not show any interest in getting back into the swing of things with dating. When men would approach her she would basically give them an application to fill out and tell them she wasn't hiring at the time. I don't think it helped any that one of her first questions was always, "Have you ever had sex with or wanted to have sex with another man?"

I'd been getting depressed myself whenever I looked through my closet lately. My clothes were beginning to either fit too tight or were out of style. Cynthia asked me to go and see Bad Boys II with Will Smith and Martin Lawrence. Normally, for this type of occasion, I'd wear a pair of jeans, a blouse, and a pair of my 3" inch sexy as hell boots, just in case I ran into someone who knew me or who wanted to know me. However, since I started dating Kyle and eating all of the elaborate meals he cooks, my ass has spread. I've gone from a perfect size ten to a close fitting twelve. So tonight I'd have to pass on the jeans, as to avoid a week spent with Monistat, and wear the cute baby blue snug fitting Baby Phat jogging suit I just purchased a few weeks ago. I pulled my hair up into a neat ponytail put on my big silver hoop earrings and matching Tiffany necklace and bracelet set. I sprayed my Romance perfume into the air and stepped into it a few times before I slipped on my Air Force One gym shoes and headed out.

We agreed to meet at the Star Theatre in Southfield by eight o'clock so that we could grab a bite to eat in one of its atrium restaurants, but it was already a quarter after seven and I still needed to stop and fill up on gas before I got onto the expressway.

I called Cynthia from my cell phone when I pulled up into the valet section in front of the theatre. She answered on the third ring, "Hello. B. Girl are you already there? Girl I'm on my way. I had a hard time getting a babysitter. His daddy cancelled on me at the last minute. It seems as if he's having second thoughts about being gay now and is upset that I'm going out. I told him that he chose to leave me for a guy, not the other way around. But, my mom came through for me and I'm on my way now. I'll be there in five minutes. I'm on Northwestern Highway. So if you want you can buy our tickets and dinner is on me."

"Damn! Slow down, I just got here myself. I haven't even gotten out of the car yet. I'm waiting for the valet guy. I'm sorry you had baby daddy drama, but you will have to calm down to hang out with me tonight. I cannot have you all high strung about some gay ass dude."

"Girl I'm cool. I am not trippin' over his ass. I'll see you in a minute."

Hanging up the phone, I rolled the window down and stuck my head out to see if the valet attendant had noticed me. He through up a finger and yelled, "Just one minute ma'am. I'll be right there."

Lying I yelled back, "Well come on then, my movie starts in three minutes."

Dealing with my impatience, he rolled his eyes, huffed and puffed a little and then ran towards my car, "I'm sorry ma'am' we're a little short staffed tonight."

"Does that mean I'll have trouble retrieving my car when I'm ready to leave this place?"

"No ma'am, not at all. I'll park it right up front and I'll make sure I get it for you as soon as you come out."

Winking at the young stud, "Thanks cutie. I'll remember that in the tip."

I stuck my phone and the valet ticket into the side pocket of my purse and briskly walked to the entrance door. It was getting a little chilly out and I wasn't wearing a jacket. The lobby was crowded as usual with teenagers playing the video games in the atrium, couples standing in the ticket line, and small families dining in the fast food restaurants. I decided to take Cynthia up on her offer to purchase dinner if I bought the tickets, so

I, too stood in line behind the happy lovers and tried to ignore their lovely dove talk and smooches. I began to wonder how many of them were on first dates. It was too bad that I wasn't on a date. I was here with a bitch, but I refused to feel sorry for myself. I looked up at the movies schedule to see the time listing for our movie. The line was moving fast so I reached into my purse and pulled out a $20 bill. I wanted to be prepared when it was my turn. I hated standing in line behind others who got up to the counter and didn't know what they wanted to see, what time they wanted to see it, or how much it cost to see it.

Just as I collected my change and the tickets, my phone rang. It was Cynthia. She was at the other end of the building and wanted to know my position. "Hold your hand up and wave or something. I'm walking that way; maybe I'll spot you."

"What color are you wearing?"

"I'm wearing a dark green jacket."

"Okay I see you. Here I come, stand still."

When I saw her we smiled and greeted each other with a hug. She had on a pair of black slacks and a sweater. Her hair was pulled back into a bun at the nape of her neck. Her hair was broken off in many spots and she felt like that hair do would cover the balding she had in the top. She didn't wear any makeup and her lips were dry and cracked. Cynthia looked bad. In fact, she looked worse to me each time we saw each other, but I chalked it up to the stress and drama going on in her life. If she lost any more weight I would definitely need to step in and purchase her a large sized combo meal from Mickey D's.

"Girl, you are going to have to start taking better care of yourself. Don't let that man bring you down,"

"What do you mean? I look that bad?"

Lying again, "No, no girl. I was just referring to the way you answered the phone earlier."

"Oh! No I'm cool. Did you get the tickets?"

"Yeah the movie starts in about 45 minutes. So what do you want to eat? I'm famished!"

"I don't know. I'm not really hungry. Maybe a salad or something."

"Let's go to Subway. I need a foot long steak and cheese. You can grab one of their salads."

"That's cool."

Watching Cynthia eat was making me feel bad about devouring my meal. She barely ate it. She picked over the lettuce and only bit into the tomatoes my once or twice.

"Cynthia what's up with you for real? When was the last time you ate?"

"Oh, I had a big lunch today. That's all, nothing to worry about. I'm good Bianca."

"Has this dude gotten you this depressed? The last time we went out you didn't touch your food and now you're barely eating this. Cynthia, I'm getting worried about you. You're losing too much weight, you're hair is falling out and your eyes are getting dark rings around them. I think you should see your physician."

"Damn Bianca, I'm fine! Let it go already."

Embarrassed and looking around to see how many people were staring at us. I sat back in my chair. "Okay Cynthia. I'm sorry calm down you're making a scene."

Now also looking around with embarrassment, she picks up her tray, throws her salad into the garbage, and says, "I'm sorry, let's just go. The movie should be starting soon. How 'bout I buy us some nachos or something."

"That sounds good to me." I wrapped up the remainder of my sandwich, put it back into the bag, and put it inside of my purse. We pushed our way through the crowd and made it to the long line at the concession stand where we stood behind a short dark skinned woman with two very light skinned children. The little girl had hazel brown eyes and long, curly, sandy brown hair. The boy's hair was cut short, but was also curly. It was obvious to all from the looks of their mulatto tone skin that their father was white. The woman glanced back at us a few times and commented on how slow the lines were moving. Cynthia and I agreed, but kept the conversation to a minimum. I exhaled fifteen minutes later when the dark woman and her children were next in line. I thought that she would put her order in and be on her way. But I was wrong.

Talking to the kids, she says, "Um, what do you guys want?" The girl responded, "I don't know, I think my dad wants a pretzel. But I want some Raisinettes."

"Bobby what do you want?"

"I want a slush and some popcorn."

She reaches down into her purse and pulls out her Visa. "Do you guys take charge cards?"

The cashier kindly responds, "Yes ma'am' we do."

"Okay, well give me two pretzels, a large popcorn, some nachos, a slush, and three lemonades."

"Um it will be a three minute wait on those pretzels."

"Three minutes, wow. Okay well just forget that and give me two hot dogs. Brianna, did you want a hot dog? Okay, make it three hot dogs."

Now I'm thinking, this bitch has been in line fifteen minutes complaining and then she gets to the front of the line and doesn't know what the fuck she wants. I began to grit my teeth and shift my weight from one leg to the other. The cashier rings up the order and proceeds to fill up the cups with the beverages. She turns to the woman and swipes the card into the card machine. "Um, I'm sorry but your card has been denied would you like to pay for your order another way?"

"Um no, I'm sorry just cancel it. Come on kids. Your dad will have to stop on the way home and get something to eat."

Unbelievable! Why do people do that shit! Cynthia and I looked at each other and laughed as the woman casually walked off. The cashier then addressed us, "May I help you?" We ordered two pretzels with cheese, two cokes, and a pack of Twizzlers and paid with cash. By the time we made it into the theatre, it was crowded, so Cynthia and I had to sit pretty close to the front. It was the only place where we could get two seats together and on the end of the aisle. That was important to Cynthia. She said that if she needed to go to the bathroom, she didn't want to climb over anyone during the movie.

Will Smith is so damn fine. Jada is one lucky broad. Gabrielle Union is one lucky broad, too. She's the one up in his arms kissing. Shit, I'm sitting here with this skinny, balding, and moody bitch. She's not even eating her pretzel and I've already eaten half of the licorice.

"Girl, you alright?"

"Yeah. I'm cool. Why?"

"Oh, no reason. This movie is pretty action packed, huh?"

"Yeah, it's pretty good. Hey, I'm going to run to the bathroom. Tell me what I missed. I'll be right back."

Looking at her strangely, I whispered back, "Okay."

She placed the remainder of her pretzel onto the floor and dashed out into the hallway of the theatre. I was beginning to think that I would have had more fun if Kyle were here. He could really get into this movie. We watched the first one together a few nights ago and I kept dozing in and out, but this one definitely has more going on in it. I had been sitting on the edge of my seat since it started.

My bladder was full and it was becoming harder for me to hold in the urine. I looked at my watch to see how much of the movie was left. Then, I began to look at the exit to see if Cynt' was returning. If I get up now, I'll probably miss the ending. "Damn!" Talking to myself, "Okay B. hold it in a few more minutes. She'll be back soon. I hope."

When the movie ended I pushed my way through the crowd exiting the theatre and rushed into the ladies room which was on the other side of the complex. There had to be about thirty stalls in the ladies room but as usual there was a short line of women waiting ahead of me. I began to do a little pee pee dance as to hold it in. When it was my turn I hurriedly covered the stool with the paper seat cover, pulled my pants and navy blue Victoria Secret thong down, plopped down on the toilet seat, and let the flood gates open. "Whew, that feels good!"

"Bianca. Is that you?"

Now a little embarrassed, "Uh, yeah. Cynt'. Is that you? You missed the end of the movie. Where were you?"

"I didn't miss it, I stood on the side and watched. My stomach is upset. I needed to vomit. So I needed to stay close to the door to make it back here."

Flushing the toilet and speaking over the running water, "Are you aw'right? Maybe you should take something. I have some Tums in my purse."

"Naw, I'm going to pick up TJ and go home. I have some Pepto Bismol there."

Looking at her strangely, I started to put the puzzle pieces together. I wanted to ask my dear friend if she was anorexic. But I decided against it as not to upset her. "Okay, I'm ready when you are just let me wash my hands. That movie was pretty good. That Will Smith is fine as hell. He's almost as cute as my sweetie."

"Almost?"

"Yeah, almost. Nobody is as sexy as my Kyle."

"Girl stop trippin'. Will's money alone is sexier than Kyle."

"Forget you. Hey, I think this is my Boo now." Looking down at my cell phone. "Oh it's my mom. What does she want?" Answering the call, "Hello."

"Bianca, where are you? Your grandma has slipped getting out of the tub. I'm on my way to the hospital can you meet me?"

"What! Yeah, Ma. I'm on my way."

BIANCA

Pulling into the parking lot of the St. John's Hospital on Moross, I rolled down my window and asked the attendant how to get to the emergency entrance. After getting the directions, I reached inside of my purse to collect the $2 dollar parking fee that he requested. He said the quickest way to the ER would be to use the skywalk on the fourth level. So I found a spot on the third level and walked over to the elevators and began to push the button frantically. "I can't believe my granny has hurt herself. Please God, let her be aw'right." Tears began to flood my eyes as I stood waiting for the elevator doors to open. I wiped my face and tried to appear calm when the bell rang and the light above the buttons lit up indicating that my ride had arrived. I stepped inside and stood next to a cute elderly couple mumbling to each other something about being new grandparents. I gave them a half smile and said, "Congratulations."

When I stepped inside of the hospital I pulled open the double doors and read the hanging signs that gave directions to the emergency waiting room. My mom was standing in the hallway, holding her cell phone and looking at the vending machines as if she was deciding on what to choose. Running up to her I yelled, "Ma what's going on? What did the doctors say? Is she alright?"

"Bianca, yeah baby, she's going to be fine. I was going to call you, but the guard just told me I couldn't use my cell phone in here. The doctor came out a few minutes ago. He said she has some bruising, but she didn't break anything. She's going to be fine. I'm waiting on her to be released now."

"Is she going home with you? Someone needs to stay with her."

"Yes, I am going to take her home with me until Monday. You know she's stubborn. She wants to get back to her own apartment. They're having a Bingo game for the senior citizens this evening."

"Mom, I feel so much better knowing she's okay. I was worried. I thought she'd really hurt herself. I was doing 80 miles per hour trying to get here. Thank God no police saw me."

Walking toward me to pull me in close, my mother hugged me, "Aw baby, you have always been a worrier. She's fine. That old bird will be around for a long time. She's not going anywhere. I'm sorry I alarmed you. I should've waited until I spoke with the doctors before I called."

"No Ma, I'm glad you called. I wasn't doing anything. I was just leaving the movies with Cynthia. Do you remember her? I went to high school with her."

"Yeah, the cute girl. She was a little thick, but she had a pretty smile."

"Yeah her. But she doesn't look all that cute anymore. She's gone through a lot over the years. She has a son now and she's a single parent. I think she's been making herself vomit after eating, too."

"Hmm, I hope not. That's dangerous. It's hard enough just trying to raise a child out here when you are by yourself. Your dad left me when you were two years old and I had to feed you, help you with homework, love you, support you, and put clothes on your back all alone. You know that man had the nerve to quit his job when the Friend of the Court began taking child support out of his checks. That fat bastard."

Now regretting bringing it up, I pulled her over to the side, "Mommie, calm down. We are in public. I know you and daddy have had some problems, but he's still my daddy and I love him. Don't bring your issues with him out and put them on me. I'm still trying to forgive him myself."

"You always did like that man. You're right though. I'm sorry."

A few minutes later two nurses wheeled my grandmother out in a chair. They were laughing and talking as though they'd known each other for years. My granny always had that affect on others. She had a beautiful personality. She was a strong woman, but was genuinely sweet and kind. She loved to talk and she laughed about everything. My granny was my heart. If anything happened to her, I would be no good to anyone.

Seeing her in that wheel chair got me all emotional so the tears began to run again. She stood up when she saw us and smiled. "Girls this is my daughter and my granddaughter, Bianca. I was telling them about you all. Yes, my Bianca is very smart. She went to college and everything."

Interrupting, I hugged her tightly and like a baby cried harder. "Granny you scared me. I told you to be more careful. You are going to be the death of me."

"Oh Bianca, girl I'm fine. Your ol' granny just slipped getting out of the shower. I've taken harder falls than this a million times in my day. There's no reason for you to shed all of these tears. Pull yourself together."

Pulling away from her and smiling, I wiped my tears away with the sleeve of my shirt. "See if I rush to your aid again. Next time I'm going to take my time getting here. Maybe I'll stop and pick up some food first."

"There won't be a next time. Your granny isn't going to take any more showers. From now on I'm just going to take a ho' bath out of the sink, throwing some water here and there."

Laughing at my grandma's antics, I walked with my mom as she pushed her in the wheelchair to the opposite end of the hospital. She'd parked in the structure on the south side of the building. My car was on the north side. I waved to my granny and told my mom that I would return the chair to the ER on my way out. Some people looked at me strangely as I walked pushing an empty chair, but I didn't care. I was just happy that everything worked out for the best with my granny.

I decided to call Kyle and let him know how things went, but recalled my mom saying that there was no cell phone usage allowed in the hospital. I began to pick up pace as to reach my exit a little faster. But, when I turned the next corner there was a large group of people leaving one of the conference rooms and I had to slow down as not to run anyone over. I imagined hearing the evening news broadcaster saying, "Woman pushing a wheelchair in the hospital was involved in a hit and run accident."

When the crowd appeared to thin out, I saw a woman who looked very familiar pointing at me while speaking to an older gentleman holding the door open for her. As I got closer, I realized that I did know her. It was Sarah. She wore a pair of orange leggings with a red and orange Coogi sweater. Her hair was pulled up into a long fake ponytail and her makeup was flawless. She was walking with a limp and using a cane to support her. But, I couldn't recall seeing her look that good in a long time.

"Sarah, is that you?"

"B. is that you?" What are you doing here? Why are you pushing that empty chair?"

"It's my grandma, she had an accident."

"Oh no, is she okay?"

"Yeah, she's fine now, I'm just taking this back to the ER. What are you doing here?'

"I'm attending an outpatient NA program here."

"NA?"

"Narcotics Anonymous. I had to get my life back after the stroke."

Now noticing her slightly impaired speech due to the mild paralysis to the right side of her face. "Yeah, I heard about that. I came to see you, but your mom refused to let me in. I'm glad to see you're doing better."

"I heard about that and I apologize for my mom's behavior. She couldn't believe how low I'd sunk to be with that man."

"Who David?"

Rolling her eyes, "Hmm yeah, David. He left me shortly after I'd gotten home from the hospital." Then holding up her right arm with her left, she said, "He couldn't handle seeing me like this."

"Where are you staying now?"

"I'm with my mom. I lost my job so I had no choice but to move back home. It's cool though I'm going to find something else."

"Are you getting the support you need through this?"

"Yeah I am. Look B. I want to apologize to you for everything I put you through."

"No Sarah. It's nothing. I know that you had no control over your actions after you started using those drugs. I still love you."

"I miss our friendship. I'm so happy to see you.

How are things with you and Kyle?"

"Good. Real good. We're working through things well."

"I heard his big dinner party for the Mayor turned out well. My mom read about it in the Metro Times. When does his restaurant open?"

"Soon. He's still working on his plans for that."

"Alright girl, that's good. Look let's exchange phone numbers and hook up again. My ride is waiting outside so I have to get going."

"Maybe it's best if I just give you my number. I don't want to call and have another run in with your mom."

Laughing a little, she said, "I understand. I don't like to have run-ins with her either."

I wrote my number down on an old paper receipt I found in my coat pocket and stuck it down in the side pocket of her purse. Then I hugged her, kissed the side of her face, and whispered in her ear, "You stay up girl."

CYNTHIA

Pulling up to my son's father's house, I had to look into my rear view mirror to prepare myself for the drama I was about to encounter. I hated fooling around with this man. I really wished he wasn't my son's father. I pulled out my Chocolate lip gloss that I'd bought from the MAC store at the mall and began to slowly smear the wand across my lips. Looking back into the mirror, I thought to myself, "This is useless, bitch. He's gay."

I threw my purse into the back seat and opened the car door. Then I raced up the stairs and pushed the bell on the door. I pulled my coat in close to fight off some of the wind that was whipping up around me. After a few minutes had passed, I began to knock on the door and then I pushed the bell again. I stepped back and looked at the window to see if any lights were on. "Come on, open the damn door. It's cold out here."

Then I heard the locks clicking and the door opened slowly. "Cynt' are you alone?"

"Yeah, why? Where's my baby? Is he ready to go?"

"Naw, he's sleeping. Come in, I'll get his coat."

Against my better judgment, I stepped into the dark Foyer and watched him disappear into the back of the house. Something felt wrong. His house isn't normally this quiet and there are usually more lights on throughout the house. "Uh, is everything okay back there?"

"No, can you come and help me get his things together."

Hesitantly, I unbuttoned my coat and followed the sound of his voice. "Where are you? I can't see a thing?"

"I'm in my room. Watch your step."

Turning the corner at the end of the hall, I stumbled and bumped my toe against a small table that held some old family photographs. Now holding my foot, I hobbled into his bedroom. "Shit! I hurt my toe. Can you turn on a light?"

"Yeah, I can. After you come over here and sit down."

"What?" Now taking my attention away from my toe to focus on him as he turned on the small lamp on the night stand. "Oh my god! What are you doing?" "I'm fixing things between us. Cynt' I can't take this anymore. I'm not sure what's going on with me. I love you and my son. I want us back."

Picking up our sleeping son and holding him tightly in my arms, I carefully watched as he waved the small black handgun close to his head. "You are gay. You chose to sleep with ol' dude. What do you mean by you want us back? That can never happen."

"Cynt' I was confused. But I am not gay. That dude just sucked my dick a few times. I am not gay. Baby, let's just start over. We could be good together."

"What are you going to do with that gun?"

"I don't know, baby. Maybe I'll kill myself or..or maybe I kill all of us. That way we can be together forever."

"You're being irrational and you are scaring me and the baby. Put it down. We can talk about this without using a gun."

"Are you saying we can get back together? Are you saying we can work this out, Boo?"

Pulling the baby closer to my chest to calm him from crying. "I am saying put the gun down. We can talk without it. Shh, shh baby. It's okay. Momma is here." Then, focusing my attention back on his dad who was now walking toward us putting the gun under his chin. "Cynt' say you'll take me back or I swear I'm going to pull this trigger."

"Put the gun down, this is not funny. You're really scaring me!"

"Cynt' I'm not pla.." POP POP

"Oh my God! No! Oh God no!"

As I watched his body drop slowly onto the bed, I dropped my baby, stood and ran to the corner of the room. Then turned to see my baby lying on the bed screaming as his father's blood slowly crept across the sheets toward him. I ran back to the bed and picked him up. Then I ran out onto the porch and down the stairs. I fell on the last two steps and cut my right calf. I felt the blood soak through my pants, but ignored it as I fumbled around in my coat pocket for my keys to unlock the doors. I put the baby in his car seat and frantically dialed 911 from my cell phone once I was inside of the car.

I sat there for the next thirty minutes waiting on the police to arrive. The emergency operator stayed on the phone with me, but I could barely hold it to my ear. I stared at the opened front door of my baby daddy's house and cried until my eye ducts ran dry. My hands were shaking and I was trembling all over. I had just witnessed the man I once thought was my soul mate accidentally take his life.

By the time the police arrived, I was in a paralyzed state of mind. My baby had cried himself back to sleep after an hour and I sat lifeless waiting on someone to wake me from what seemed like a horrible dream.

“Ma'am," taping on the window, the EMS driver motioned for me to push the button and unlock the doors. “Ma'am I'm going to open the door and help you. We need to check you and the baby. Okay, I need you to slowly step out of the car. The police have arrived and everything is okay now. Everything is going to be all right. Please come with me.”

Sitting in the back of the truck, I had a flash back of everything and began to cry all over again. The attendant who was checking my blood pressure put her arms around me and held me tight.

Two of the police officers crowded around me and asked if there was anyone they could call for me. They wanted to ask me more questions about the shooting, but I just didn't have it in me to answer at the time. The female officer began scrolling through the numbers on my cell phone and spoke softly, "Okay Cynthia I know you're a little upset right now. So I am going to call someone for you. Is that okay if I call your mom for you? Hmm, Cynthia would that be all right? I am going to have her pick up the baby and were going to need you to come with us for questioning."

The emergency technician offered me some tissue to wipe my face as she cut my bloody right pant leg to examine my now swollen calf. As she cleaned the wound I watched as and two of the other EMTs rolled his body out of the house and down the steps. The female police officer then escorted me to her squad car. My baby and I rode with her to the police station where my mom met us and handled everything from that point on.

BIANCA

The funeral for Cynthia's son's father was held three days later at his mother's church. It was a closed casket ceremony. The church was packed with young and old people who all had nice things to say about him. Apparently no one knew or no one spoke on his shady affair with the brother who sat in the back of the church wearing dark shades. Cynthia had pointed him out to me as we passed him coming into the sanctuary. "Girl that's him wearing that navy blue Versace suit and tie."

"Damn! Oops, I mean dang he's cute. Ooh and look at his shoulders. He's all sexy. Why does he have to be gay?"

"Well, what can I say? You know how good a dick can be."

Trying not to snicker at her last comment, I covered my mouth and turned my head. His mom was wearing a beautiful black silk dress with silver jewelry accents. She was sitting on the front row next to his dad, grandparents, and siblings. She didn't really look Cynt' in the eyes when we greeted her to give our condolences. She shook both of our hands and thanked Cynthia for allowing TJ to spend time with her the night before. She was pleasant, but it was still obvious that there was some tension between the two of them. Cynthia later told me that while his mom didn't totally blame her for leaving her son, she did feel as though Cynt' could have somehow prevented his death.

I asked Kyle to prepare a few cakes to take to her house after the burial. I offered to go with my friend for support and I had her back in case any of his family members felt froggy enough to jump her. But, when we arrived everyone was cordial, that is until his older sister got there and began "mean mugging" us. She sat in the corner of the living room and slowly ate her chicken while mumbling obscenities at us.

"Cynt' you want me to get her out back. We can beat that bitch. You hit her and I'll stomp her once she's down."

"Do you really think that would be a good idea? We are here with her peeps. We'd have to fight everybody in here just to make it out alive."

"Yeah, you're right. But if I catch her out in public, it's on."

"Thanks."

"Oh anytime, girl. Anytime."

After about twenty more minutes had passed, Mrs. Jones's house was packed with mourners. Some were crying while others chose to honor his memory with laughter. They told happy stories about his childhood and teenage years. I gathered around a few of the happier crowds while Cynthia met with Tim's parents in the den. I kept one eye on the opened door my friend had entered and the other on the crazy sister that had been threatening us. That is until my bladder began to beg me for mercy and I had to run to the half bathroom, which was located in the back of the house next to the kitchen.

"Okay Cynthia, you're on your own for now, but I'll be back."

The small restroom was decorated with beautiful shades of blue with white trimmings. I was impressed with what she'd done in such a tight space. There were candles and apple scented potpourri in a dish on the back of the toilet and cute little hand towels neatly folded on a towel rack that was mounted on the back of the door. The small white pedestal sink had silver plated handles and the plush blue rugs on the floor felt like heaven.

"Good job Mrs. Jones. This bathroom is nice!"

Normally I would be nervous about using a stranger's bathroom, but this was nice. Upon exiting the john, I was approached by Tim's sisters. I immediately put on my "please don't fuck with me today" face and cautioned the women on how I was feeling.

"Today would not be a good day for you all to come at me like this. Whatever beef you may have with Cynthia needs to be squashed until after your family members have mourned your brother's death."

Then the light skinned, short one spoke, "You

mean his murder. That bitch murdered our brother. She may not have pulled the trigger, but she's responsible for him acting the way he did."

"Okay and you're telling me this for what?"

Now the other one spoke, "Oh bitch, don't get smart. We'll beat yo' ass along with hers just for being here with her."

"Humph, you think so, huh?" Taking off my shoes and sitting my purse down on the floor, I pulled off my earrings and welcomed the challenge. "Don't let all of this pretty shit fool you. I am not going to back down, if you two think you can beat my ass, bring it." When I stood back up from placing my jewelry in my purse, I pulled out my pepper spray and caught both of them in the face. I pushed the short one, kicked her in the stomach, and then I turned on her sister and began to rapidly punch her in the face.

All of the commotion and screams prompted some of the gentlemen to rush to their aid. It took two of Tim's uncles to pull me off of the older sister. The younger one couldn't handle the beat down and ran after I'd torn her blouse. The older one caught me with a few blows so my lip was bleeding, but overall I must say I handled my own.

Mrs. Jones allowed me to collect my things before she asked Cynthia and I to leave. I was escorted out to the car, but she was able to walk out on her own. She was embarrassed by my actions and apologized several times before she and TJ joined me outside.

"Why did you do that? Bianca that was

completely uncalled for. What are you doing? Oh my God! How could you do that?"

"What? Those bitches tried to jump me! They approached me coming out of the bathroom. I can't believe you're questioning me like this. What the fuck? I'm the innocent bystander. I don't know these broads. I'm here with you. I came to watch your back."

Staring at me with amazement, she asked, "What happened in there?"

"I just kicked their asses. That's what happened!"

She sat silently for a minute and then she smiled, "Bitch, you are crazy."

Examining my swollen and busted lip in the mirror, I placed the ice cubes she brought out in a Ziploc sandwich bag against my mouth. "I'm not crazy. I'm a survivor. Man, I'm from the eastside. Where were you?"

Now laughing out loud as we turned the corner, "I was talking with his mom and dad. They want to set up a college fund for TJ. Apparently, she had a big life insurance policy on Tim. They say they want to help me and do as much as they can for their grandson. He's all they have to remember his dad by."

"That's cool. Girl, I'm sorry."

"Don't be sorry. I didn't like them bitches anyway. I'm glad you beat them up."

"Yeah, well I could have used your help."

"Trust me, from the looks of things, they're the ones who needed help."

BIANCA

UNDER THE WEATHER

Michigan weather sucks! Last week the temperature was up to seventy-two degrees. This week we have rain and the temperature is now a chilly forty-five degrees. I don't know which coat or clothes to wear from day to day. Now I have this horrible head cold and I missed my two -week hair appointment. Shit! I really needed to see that girl this week. It's definitely time for a touch up. My new growth appears to be three inches long and I am not going to begin to talk about how tight the naps are on the back of my neck.

I had to miss work today. I hated calling in, too. I had to use my last sick day. But, my head was pounding and I couldn't breathe to save my life when the alarm clock went off this morning. I rolled out of bed slowly, crept into the bathroom, and brushed my teeth. I swallowed the last teaspoon of Nyquil and made myself some lemon tea. Then, I grabbed a roll of toilet tissue out of the linen closet and curled up on the couch with my electric blanket. After flipping through the channels for about thirty minutes I dozed off into a semi comatose sleep. That is until I heard someone's car alarm going off out in the parking lot. Normally, I would get up and look out of the window, but today I couldn't care less. I scooted down further under the cover and adjusted the pillows. If it's my car I'll just report it stolen later.

After disturbing me for a few more minutes, the alarm stopped. But then I could hear two of my neighbors chatting loudly in the hallway with one another.

"Eh man, did you see that game on Sunday?"

"Naw man, my girl was tripping, so I had to spend some time with her. I missed the whole thing. Who won?"

"We did. It was a good game too! The Lions are trying to do something this year."

"Aw, I hate I missed it now."

"Yeah well, I am having a few guys over this week. Stop by and hang out if you can get out."

Now stomping down the remainder of stairs and yelling back, *"Yeah aw'right man. I'll be there."*

I was glad that was over, if it had gone on any longer I would've opened the door and told the both of them to shut the hell up. The Matlock rerun that I was half watching was almost over, so I turned up the volume to hear his closing remarks. It always trips me out when he pulls out the smallest piece of incriminating evidence and wins each and every trial. If I were the killers I'd knock his ass off first and then go for the person who pissed me off.

I sat up to blow my nose again and place the used tissue on top of the others that began to pile up on the end of the table. Then I tore off another small piece, folded it neatly and stuck it into my right nostril before I lay down again. The skin below my nose was red and dry. I now wished I had spent those few extra dollars and bought that soft tissue with the lotion in it. I hated being sick!

After unsuccessfully getting back into that coma like sleep on my couch, I turned off my blanket and decided to get back in bed. I poured myself a glass of OJ and toasted a cinnamon raisin bagel. The cream cheese that had been sitting in my fridge looked funny. So, when it popped up, I buttered it, put the tissue box under my arm, and carried my small breakfast in each hand. I stopped at the thermostat outside of my bedroom door and adjusted the heat a little, then proceeded on to my queen-sized boyfriend (the nickname for my bed) who was calling out my name. I pulled back his down filled shirt, fluffed his pecks, and climbed on top of him. He hugged me back and whispered in my ear, "I'll take good care of you, baby." He knows what I like to hear.

Three hours into his good loving my phone rang and startled me. I jumped up quickly and hit the snooze button on the alarm clock. When the ring sounded again, I realized my mistake and grabbed the phone from the night stand.

"Hello."

"Baby are you okay? I called you at work and I didn't get an answer."

Trying to sound sexy, I cleared my throat and pretended to feel better, "Hey Kyle, baby. Yeah, I'm fine. I just have a small cold."

"A small cold, huh? Bianca you sound like your head is going to explode. What are you taking?"

"I took some Nyquil and drank some tea. I'll be fine. Don't fuss over me."

"I'm coming over. Have you eaten?"

"Yeah, I had a bagel and juice. Baby I'm fine."

"So you don't want me to come over?"

"Of course I do. But I'm fine really don't make a big deal. I just need to rest."

"I'll be there as soon as I can."

I hung up the phone, took a shower, and put on the pink cotton pajama short set my grandma had bought for me months ago. I didn't bother to put on any panties because I didn't know how things would happen once Kyle showed up. It had been a while since we'd spent time together, so cold or no cold, I wanted some dick. I quickly hung up some of the clothes that I had neglected to hang up during the week. When I was finished, I checked the medicine cabinet for some Tylenol to help fight off the headache that was now kicking me in the ass, but the bottle was empty. "Shit!" I threw it in the trash and stomped back into the bedroom. "Maybe if I just lie here quietly until he arrives I'll feel better."

Another hour had passed and I realized that my assumption was wrong. I didn't feel better at all. When Kyle rang the buzzer I didn't move. I couldn't move. It was fine though. I knew he would use his key when I didn't answer.

He didn't say anything right away. I guess he thought I was sleeping and he didn't want to disturb me. I heard him doing some things up front and after a few minutes I could smell the aroma of food cooking in the kitchen. When he entered the room, he had a serving tray with a small pot and a towel on it. There was hot steam and the smell of Vicks Vapor Rub in the air. He sat the tray at the end of the bed and rubbed my back softly.

"Bianca, you awake?"

"Yeah, I'm awake. What do you have?"

"Something that should help you out. My mom used to do this for me when I was coming up. Sit up, you have to hold this towel over your head and let the steam hit you in the face."

"Is this Vicks in here?"

"Yeah, it's hot water and Vicks Vapor Rub. I boiled it. If this doesn't open your head up, nothing will."

"What are you cooking?"

"I'm making you some chicken noodle soup. I got you some Theraflu tea in there, too. I'm going to fix you up. You'll be up and feeling real good by this weekend."

Removing the towel, and looking up, "What's going on this weekend?"

Wiping the tears from my eyes, "We're taking a trip."

"A trip? Kyle I can't go anywhere. I used my last vacation day today so I need to be at work Friday."

"You will be able to go to work Friday and Monday. We're just doing a quick getaway. We leave Friday night and we'll be back Sunday."

Now smiling, "Where are we going?"

"I see you're feeling better, huh. Yeah, I can tell by that pretty smile."

"Stop being silly. Where are we going?"

"Viva Las Vegas, Baby!"

I threw the towel onto the floor, grabbed him around the neck, and hugged him tight. "Ah, baby are you serious? Can you get time off?"

Kissing my neck, he pulled me close and nibbled on my ear, "Yeah, I took the time off. I haven't been able to spend time with you lately and you have been so good about everything that's been going on with the business and Tamara, it's time for me to focus some attention on us."

"You know that's my spot. Your making me wet, baby stop. I want to know more about this trip."

Placing his hand on my thigh and slowly inching his way up, "I thought this was your spot." Now placing his index finger inside of my shorts and tickling my clitoris, "Oh you are wet, maybe I was wrong. I've been nibbling on the wrong spot all of this time."

"You always nibble on the right spots." Closing my eyes, I allowed him to have his way with me.

He took my shirt off and began to suckle my breast. "Baby have you missed me?"

"Hell yeah. Can't you tell?"

Making reference to my hard nipples, "I thought you were just cold."

Pushing him away, "I see you have a lot of jokes today."

"I'm just feeling good baby. I'm feeling real good." Clapping his hands and doing a silly dance, he pulled me up into his arms and carried me into the living room, "Come on let's go. I rented a movie and you need to eat this soup. I got to get you back on your feet. We're going to Vegas baby! We've got to hang out at the Hoover Dam, club hop, shop, and check out the sights."

Unbuttoning his shirt and nibbling on his ear, I whispered, "I need to check these sights out first." I sucked on his neck a little and wiggled my way out of his arms. I got down on my knees and took his brown Coach belt loose and unzipped his pants with my teeth. Then, I slowly pulled his pants down below his calves with one hand and found his erect penis with the other. I freed my friend from its tight hold inside of Kyle's sports boxers and placed it inside of my mouth. I pretended to swallow and took it in a little further. When I looked up at my lover, his eyes were closed and he was pleased. He gently rubbed the back of my neck and moaned loudly. His knees began to shake and he was weak. I smiled. "Not yet baby. Don't come yet. I need to feel you inside of me."

He joined me on the carpet and pulled at my shorts aggressively. He entered me quickly and moved fast. I screamed out his name several times and begged him not to cum. I could feel the skin on the small of my back begin to burn from the carpet fibers rubbing against me. And then it happened. We both reached our climax at the same time. I felt his warm sperm move inside of me and I welcomed it. He grabbed my face and kissed me softly. I sucked on his tongue and then pulled away breathing rapidly. "Baby, I love you."

"I love you, too!"

BIANCA

By Friday morning I was on cloud nine. My head cold had cleared up and with the exception of a few sniffles. I had my hair and nails done the night before. My clothes were packed and I was able to make it to the work for the rest of the week. I got a lot accomplished, too! I had phoned my mom to let her know Kyle and I would be away this weekend. I had even gone so far as to change the message on my voice mail to let others know, too.

Yeah, you've reached Bianca, unfortunately I can't answer this call, but if you leave a message I'll call you when I get back from Vegas. Thanks, bye!

This weekend is going to be real good for us. I haven't had a chance to really enjoy my man since we'd become an official couple. He'd been busy with work, Tamara, and setting up his affairs for the business. I had been working and hanging out with Cynthia. But over the next few days, I planned to really put it down for my Boo. I stopped by Lover's Lane on my way home and purchased a few items. I had two new sexy lingerie sets; one red silk teddy with lace crouchless panties, and the other was a long black shear gown with matching bra and panties. I had also purchased a long blond wig, a pair of three inch "fuck me hard" pumps and a latex dress. I'm into role-playing. I made a quick chef salad and poured myself a glass of diet Pepsi. I sat down at the kitchen table and flipped through my mail. There was a large brown envelope from my mom, a few bills, and some catalogs from Sears and Victoria's Secret. I opened the one from my mom first. She said that I had received some mail at her house and that she'd forward it to me. I didn't expect it to be much, probably just some junk mailings. There were some postcard invites to upcoming cabarets, a pre-approved credit offer, and a purple envelope with a familiar handwriting on the front. It just read, "To Bianca H." I opened it slowly. I didn't know what to expect. It was a card from Chauncey, so I was excited but a little nervous. It was one of those sappy love cards with a beautiful picture of a black couple sitting on a beach together. The front of the card read, "I'm missing you an all of those special moments we spent together." On the inside there was a short poem speaking on mistakes and miscommunications and it ended with an apology. He signed it, "Let's give us another try, and Love you, Chauncey."

I read it twice and smiled. I was really flattered, but he had let too much time pass for forgive and forgets. I had moved on to someone new. I considered saving the card to read on one of those days that I was feeling blue, but decided against it. I admired the picture of the couple one more time and tossed into the garbage with the remainder of my unwanted salad.

I hung up my work clothes and placed a pair of blue Capri jeans and a sweater on the bed. I turned on the hot water in the shower and wrapped my hair up. I considered taking a quick nap after the warm water had soothed my nerves, but the clock on my nightstand argued against it. I had just enough time to do some last minute packing and get dressed. Kyle was sending a Metro car to pick me up and it would be here soon.

The driver rang the buzzer just as I'd zipped up my boots. I gave myself one last glance over before grabbing my luggage and running out. I raced down the stairs and out into the street in record time. Nothing was going to interfere with this weekend. The driver put my things into the trunk of the black Oldsmobile and we were off. I started to call Kyle from my cell, but I decided to save my minutes. We were to meet each other at the terminal, so I'd just call once I got closer to the airport.

It only took the driver about twenty-five minutes once we got onto I-94. There weren't many cars out, so it was a clear shot. I thanked Bill and tipped him for his service and pleasant conversation. He offered to carry my bags inside, but I declined. Once inside, I approached the short line of people waiting at the Northwest ticket counter. I pulled out my cell and dialed Kyle. After the third ring his voice mail came on, so I left him a message letting him know that I had arrived and hung up. I got out of line and decided to wait for him outside of one of the restaurants in the atrium. I glanced at my watch and began to wonder what could be holding him up. He's normally very punctual.

I picked up a copy of the Jet magazine that was sitting in an empty seat nearby and flipped through a few pages when I was startled by the vibration in my purse. I fumbled through the makeup case and wallet at the bottom of my bag and found my small cell phone.

"Hello! Kyle, baby where are you? We're running late. Are you stuck in traffic or something?"

"Hey baby. No I'm not in traffic, I'm here at the hospital with Tamara. I'm afraid we're going to have to postpone our trip. She's in labor."

"WHAT? Postpone. Kyle I'm already here at the airport. Why didn't you call me sooner? My ride is gone. How am I supposed to get home?"

"Bianca, I'm sorry. Her mom called me about fifteen minutes ago. I called your house, but I didn't get an answer. Can you call Cynthia or your mom and have one of them pick you up?"

"Kyle this is some bullshit! Is this what I will have to put up with from you and this bitch? Cause baby I have gone through this type of shit before and I can't do this again."

"Bianca, she's having my baby. What else can I do? I want to be here for my child."

"Fine Kyle, you do that but don't think I'm going to continue sitting on the back burner for this bitch. I'll call somebody to pick me up don't worry about it."

"B. don't do this. You know I can't abandon my kid. I promise I'm going to make this up to you. Baby I love you, don't be an"

I closed the phone shut in the midst of his apology. A few people who were close by stared at me curiously. I sat down and rested my head in the palms of my hands and cried. I don't believe this shit is happening all over again. My man is going to be someone else's baby's daddy. What the fuck? I wiped the tears from my eyes and began to pull myself together. I opened my phone and scrolled down the list of names until I found Cynthia's home phone number. Before I pushed the little green button to dial her up, I mumbled under my breath, "I'm sorry, too Kyle, but I can't do this again."

KYLE

WILL THE REAL DADDY PLEASE STAND UP!

Pushing the button on the elevator to the maternity ward made me feel strange. A few months ago I was a single and lonely man getting over Tamara and now I'm going to be a father. I was elated! I shifted the huge teddy bear and balloons I'd purchased at the hospital gift store to my right and eased into the elevator doors. There were a few other proud papas and families waiting to get in as well. Just as we'd all gotten settled inside and the doors were closing, a short browned skinned guy stuck his foot inside and yelled, "Hold it please." So I reached out to assist and pushed the "door open" button.

"Thanks man."

"No problem."

Admiring my oversized stuffed animal, he turned and said, "You're a proud dad to be, huh?"

"Yeah, my girl - I mean my ex-girlfriend is having my baby."

"Huh, join the club. My ex is up here, too. She

went into labor a few hours ago. I rushed over here as soon as I could. We're having a boy."

"That's cool. We are, too."

"Congratulations."

The doors opened and we all piled out just as quickly as we'd piled in. Some of us entered the waiting room, a few of us walked directly into the birthing rooms, and the guy I'd spoken to on the way up and I approached the nurses desk to inquire about our loved ones. Well in my case, to inquire about Tamara. I wouldn't necessarily call her a loved one. She was a borderline hated one.

I stood behind the short guy and waited my turn to question the young attendant behind the counter. She greeted him with a friendly smile and asked if she could assist him. He smiled back, put his Mack on, complimented her beauty and inquired about her dating status. She turned him down politely before asking him again who he was there to see.

"Tammy. I mean Tamara Pickett."

At the sound of her name, I stepped up to listen more closely. The nurse questioned further, "Is that your girlfriend?"

"Uh no, she's my ex-girlfriend. So I guess you could just call her my soon to be son's mother."

"You mean she's your baby's mama?"

Now annoyed by her sarcasm, he turned side ways and spoke nonchalantly, "Yeah, I guess you could say that. What room, please?"

"Oh she's in room 525. Take this hallway all the way around. The numbers are on the doors.

The doctor just went in to see her."

"Thank you, pretty girl."

Stepping aside, I was devastated and a little confused. Tamara told me that I was the father. I'd spent all of this time and money on her with Lamaze classes, maternity clothes, and baby supplies. Who was this dude? Where had he been these last few months? I wanted to stop him and ask questions, but I didn't know how he rolled or what he was 'bout. So I decided to just chill and lay in the cut for a while. I gave the gifts to the attendant and asked her to deliver them to Tamara after the baby was born. Then, I went downstairs and sat in the main lobby to collect my thoughts.

I watched people come in and out of the large rotating doors and quickly fell into a semi-depression. I walked over to the coffee and donut vendor that was set up near the entrance and purchased a cup of black decaf. I picked up a copy of the Metro Times and reclaimed my spot on the worn down black leather couch. I attempted to take my mind off things by sipping the hot fluid and reading the different articles. It was beginning to work, too that is until I heard my mom calling out my name.

"Kyle. Kyle baby! I'm over here! I'm here baby. Where is she?"

Looking up from my magazine to acknowledge that I heard her cry, I stood to greet her "Hey, Ma. She's upstairs."

Rambling on, "Is the baby here yet? What are

you doing down here? Why aren't you watching the birth of your child? Is Bianca here with you?"

Now remembering Bianca, whom I left at the airport and feeling even worse, "No mom, she isn't with me. I'm here alone. I rushed over when Tamara's mom called me."

"Well why aren't you up there with her?"

"Mom, please stop with the questions. I'm not with Tamara because there's another guy up there claiming he's the father of that baby."

Pausing and standing quietly before hugging me tightly. "Son, I'm sorry. I didn't know. What is she saying about this?"

"I don't know. I haven't seen her yet. The nurse said that the doctor had just gone in to see her. So, I came down here to think this out."

"Say no more. Son, I'm going up there right now. In the meantime, you call Bianca; she should be here with you. If you're going to marry her, you two need to think this through together."

Hugging my mom again, I kissed her face and gave her the directions up to the maternity ward. She was right, I had shut Bianca out of this part of my life and that was wrong. If this child is mine and Bianca is whom I intend to marry she needs to take part in this. I knew I was going to have some serious ass kissing to do. I walked over to the payphone and dialed her cell phone. She answered on the second ring and said, "Kyle, it's over. I can't do this anymore. It's obvious that Tamara and that baby are important to you right now and you need time to focus on that. So..."

Taking a deep breath before I interrupted her spew of words, “B. the baby isn’t mine! Well, I don’t know if it is or not. There’s another guy here claiming to be her ex and the baby’s daddy. I’m sorry about earlier. I didn’t mean to dismiss you like I did. Baby I need you. I love you Bianca and you’re the woman I want to be with. If..”

Now cutting me off, “Kyle I love you, too but I don’t want any drama in my life and it seems as though this girl is full of it. You need to get a paternity test. I’m going to have Cynthia bring me to you and we’re going to settle all of this bullshit once and for all.”

After speaking to me in that stern manner, the phone went dead. She’d hung up the phone just as quickly as she’d answered it. I placed the receiver back into the cradle, discarded my trash and proceeded back up to the maternity ward. My plan was to follow Bianca’s directions.

When I reached Tamara’s room, the door was shut and my mom and the short guy were pacing back and forth. When she saw me, she stopped and grabbed the guy by the arm.

“This is my son Kyle. Kyle this is Greg. Gregory Packer.” We nodded and spoke, “What’s up?”

“Kyle, Gregory says that Tamara moved in with him after she left you. They’d been living with each other up until the time she showed up again claiming to be pregnant with your child. He says that he just recently lost his job and after finding out, Tamara moved back home with her mom. He believes that baby is his, but is willing to do a blood test and split the cost with you. What do you think?"

"Mom have you been interrogating this man?"

"No. We've just been having a friendly conversation while that witch is in there having the baby. He couldn't watch and I was too pissed to stay in there, so we stepped out here and introduced ourselves."

Turning to Greg, I reached out to shake his hand. "Yeah man, I'm sorry about all of this. I'm cool with the test if you are. I just need to get all of this mess settled. If this isn't my baby, I don't want Tamara to ever contact me again."

"Dude I hear dat. She's a trip. I know. I want to be a good father to my child, that is if it's mine, but I don't want to be bothered with her lying ass anymore either."

We spoke for a few more minutes before the door to her room opened. The doctor stepped out into the hall and spoke quietly. He shook Greg's hand and congratulated him on having a beautiful nine-pound baby boy. He looked at me and smiled, then before walking away he patted my back and asked if I were the uncle. I didn't know how to respond. So I said, "No, I think I'm one of the proud dads." That stopped him in his tracks. He turned around slowly and apologized.

"I'm sorry. Will you two be needing a DNA test done?"

"Yes, I think we do."

Greg stepped up and spoke, "Uh Doc., I'm

sorry about all of this, but that won't be necessary." Looking at him seriously, I spoke, "Yeah we do. She's been playing the both of us. She doesn't know who the father is. Man, what are you doing?"

"I want to talk with her first. I think she'll tell us the truth. She doesn't really have a choice now. We're both here. I say we go in there, look at the baby, and ask her point blank. It beats spending our money on a test."

My mom nodded in agreement. The doctor stood silently waiting on our decision. Greg was ready to open the door and confront the one person who had the power to change both our lives, but I was hesitant. What if the baby wasn't mine? What if he was?

Either way I had to make a decision. "What the hell, man. Let's go in."

He pushed the door open and we entered. Tamara's mom was sitting near the window on the telephone. She was informing all of their relatives of the new addition to the family. Tamara was holding the baby and attempting to breast feed him. The nurse stood above her attentively waiting to offer her assistance. When she turned to acknowledge who'd entered the room, her mouth fell open and she looked as if she'd just witnessed a double homicide. "Greg. Uh, Kyle what are you doing here?"

"What do you mean? Your mom called me. She said that you were having our son, so I rushed over."

Now showing the puzzled expression on his face. Greg jumped in, "Yeah baby, she called me, too." Then without skipping a beat he asked, "Who is this baby's father, Tamara?"

Taking notice of the tone in his voice, the nurse offered to take the baby to the nursery. Tamara's mom hung up the phone and stood next to her now obviously nervous daughter. Giving the baby to the nurse, she adjusted her breast and closed her gown before responding. "I see the two of you have met." Turning to her mother, she reached out for her hand. "I knew this would all catch up with me at some point. I don't really know how to explain my actions and I want to apologize to the both of you for what I've done. When I realized that I was pregnant I was afraid. I was afraid and nervous. Who would have ever thought that I could be someone's mother?" Now wiping the tears from her eyes and licking her trembling lips. "Greg this is your son. I only told Kyle it was his because you'd just lost your job and I didn't think you could help me support this child like he could. Kyle you're a good man. I knew you'd do the right thing even if you didn't want to be bothered with me, but the truth is I knew I was pregnant with Greg's baby a month before I left you. That's why I stopped having sex with you and moved in with him. I had been cheating on you with Greg for months."

My mom walked up and rubbed my back to console my broken heart and hurt feelings. I stepped back slowly and turned to exit the room.

Then, I stopped and shook Greg's hand, "Congratulations man, and good luck." I looked back at my ex-girlfriend who was now sobbing in her mother's arms. I walked over to the bed, sat down, and held her hand. "Tamara I would have given you the world. You and this child, had it been mine. All I can do now is thank you for coming clean and telling the truth. I will eventually forgive you for all of this, but it will never be forgotten. I pray in Jesus' name that you get yourself together, if not for yourself then for this child. He deserves it. He didn't ask to be here. I wish you all the luck. You take care."

After speaking my peace, I stood up, grabbed my mom by the hand and we left. I didn't look back again. I felt good about what I said and I was ready to move on with my life. I met Bianca down in the lobby. She was coming through the swinging doors as I was getting my mom's parking ticket validated. She greeted my mother with that beautiful smile and they kissed each other's faces. We both informed her of everything that went on with the baby and Tamara. She didn't seem to be too surprised. She took it all pretty well. I knew I had been blessed with something great. It was the love of a wonderful feisty woman. After seeing my mother off, I turned to my queen, picked her up off of her feet, and held on to her real tight. "Baby it's all over now."

BIANCA

Kyle surprised me two weeks later with another offer to take a small vacation together. This time we were headed for Miami to take a small weekend cruise to the Bahamas. We were doing it big too. He was taking me on the Royal Caribbean cruise line. We had a suite on the promenade deck with a beautiful seaside view.

I packed a few simple cotton dresses, sandals, and three bathing suits. I opted for braids so that I wouldn't have to bring along any hot curlers. I had plans on outdoing Stella on this trip. She did make Jamaica look good, but I was going to make this Bahama trip look a whole lot better.

I showered and changed into my black evening gown for our dinner with the captain. I pinned my braids up into an elegant ball at the nape of my neck and put on the gold omega necklace I'd purchased at Marshall Field's a few days before. I slid on my black three inch pumps and admired my own pedicure. I sprayed my Happy perfume into the air and stepped into the falling midst. I gave myself one last look over in the mirror and blew a kiss.

"Are you admiring yourself?"

Turning towards my beau embarrassed by my conceit. "Yes I am. Aren't I allowed to think wonderful thoughts about myself?"

"Just as long as you admire me, too."

"Oh baby you know I always do that." I reached out for his hand and pulled him in close. "Thanks again for this trip baby, this is great!"

Kissing my forehead and then rubbing my nose with his, he spoke, "No thank you for agreeing to come with me. I thought that you would never speak to me again after everything that went on with Tamara. I love you baby. Thanks for hanging in there with me."

Now sliding my tongue into his mouth, I closed my eyes and enjoyed the moment. He pulled away slowly and smiled at me. "What are you doing?"

"I'm enjoying you. The way you smell, feel, and taste. You're not bad on the eyes either. What do you say we skip dinner and feast on each other for a while? We can grab a bite to eat at the midnight buffet tonight."

"No. I don't want us to spend the entire trip having sex. We're going to get out of this room and see everything we can on this trip."

"What? Are you serious? Come on baby. Don't deny me my little friend."

"Hey, don't refer to him as little. Don't you know that guys hate that?"

Giggling at him I rubbed my friend and assured him that I was completely satisfied with its size. "I'm sorry, I didn't mean it that way. You're right, let's get out of here. I'm feeling lucky. Let's hit the casino before dinner."

"Okay, just let me freshen up a little."

He took his jacket off, laid it across the mini bed, and went into the bathroom. I kicked my shoes off and sat on the corner of the bed. I reached out for the television remote and turned on the tube. I heard the water in the bathroom sink running and assumed Kyle was brushing his teeth.

"Hey, baby what do you think about going into the bar later for Karaoke. I think I feel like singing tonight."

"@#%%% $%^"

"What? I didn't understand a word you said."

I pushed the mute button on the remote and leaned forward towards the small restroom door and accidentally slid his suit jacket onto the floor. "Oh shit."

I picked up the jacket and brushed it off quickly. I hoped it didn't get wrinkled. I returned it to its previous position and sat down innocently. I heard the water stop so I decided to put my shoes back on and get my things together. I went to the closet and grabbed my shawl, through some lipstick and a few dollars into my purse, and began to search for my shoes. I found one close to where I'd taken it off near the bed, but the other decided to take a small trip of its own under the bed. I knelt down carefully as not to tear my stockings and felt around on the floor for my heel.

I yelled out to Kyle who was still inside of the bathroom, "Baby are you almost ready, we're running out of time?" Just then, I felt my shoe and pulled it out into view. Something was different about it. It felt heavier and the black box that sat inside of it changed its style. I looked at it sideways and tried to catch my breath. It must have fallen from Kyle's jacket. I removed the box and opened it slowly. "Oh my God. Oh Lord." I jumped up and down and did a short dance before taking the huge diamond ring out and sliding it onto my finger. "YES!" It looked real good with my French manicured nails.

"I see you like the ring."

Startled by his presence, I screamed and turned around to face him. "Oh baby, are you sure about this?" Smiling from ear to ear, I apologized for finding it and tried to explain myself. I must have looked like a kid with my hand stuck in the cookie jar. "Oh my God, baby it's beautiful."

He smiled at me and approached me slowly. Then his facial expression changed and he became very serious. "Yes, I am sure about this. I love you Bianca and that ring doesn't come close to your beauty." He grabbed both of my hands and kneeled down on one knee. "Bianca Sinclair, I wanted to surprise you this evening after dinner, but since you've found it, and you're wearing it, my only job now is to ask you to accept my proposal." Then swallowing hard, he wiped the tears from my face, looked me in the eyes and spoke, "Will you marry me?"

Now crying harder, I fell onto my knees, hugged him tightly, and buried my head in his shoulders. I couldn't breathe. I couldn't speak. I didn't know what to do or how to respond. This is the day that I had been waiting for all of my life and it was finally here. This was it! This is the man that God has sent to me. This is the man that I'd have the house and two point five children with. This is the man I intended on sharing the rest of my life with, forever.

I sat back on my legs and held the sides of his face in my palms. I smiled and admired my king. I gently kissed his lips, his nose, his eyelids, and both of his cheeks. Then I held his hands in mine, looked at him lovingly, and spoke, "Yes, I will."

EPILOGUE

Kyle smiled as he paced back and forth outside of the bathroom door. He wiped the sweat from his hands onto his pant legs and knocked at the large wooden wall that stood between him and his new wife, Bianca.

"Baby, what's going on in there?"

"Kyle, give me a few more seconds."

After being baptized, Bianca began taking the new member classes along with the marriage courses that were offered at Kyle's church. She quit her job at Ford and became the third partner in SINCLAIR'S. Business at their restaurant was flourishing and the happy couple wanted to focus more attention on building their family so that one-day they could pass their empire down to their offspring. So, she had given up her birth control pills, and the newlyweds had been consummating their marriage everyday for two months. Her cycle was now two weeks late.

She'd picked up one of those home tests from the drug store and Kyle was anxious about his real opportunity at being a proud papa.

"Okay Bianca, you should see something now.

What does it say? Are we pregnant or what?"

Opening the door slowly, she stepped into the bedroom with her lover. Her head hung low. "Um, Kyle baby I'm sorry but the results aren't good." She covered her face with her hands and approached him pretending to sob uncontrollably.

Disappointed, he reached out for his spouse to console her. "Baby, it's okay. It's just not our time yet. You have to believe and put your trust in the Lord. He's going to bless us. I know it."

Pushing him away, Bianca laughed abruptly and yelled, "I know it, too Kyle because He already has. I couldn't tell you the results were good because." Now mocking Tony the Tiger in the Frosted Flakes commercial, she swung her arm into the air as she said, "They're GREAT!"

"What?"

"Baby, we're having a baby!

Looking into her eyes seriously, he repeated her last statement. "We're having a baby. Oh my goodness. Bianca. Stop playing. Are we really?" He rushed past his wife, who was laughing hysterically on the floor while hitting the plush beige carpet with her hands. He picked up the EPT stick which displayed the GREAT news. Holding back his tears, he lowered his head and closed his eyes. He recalled the sermon on Hosea that his pastor had delivered and said a small prayer. "Thank you Father for another great blessing. I have always tried to follow your commands and I promise to love Bianca and this child for all the days of my life. Amen."

VALUABLE LESSONS TAUGHT IN "NO MORE MISS B. HAVIN"

1. **Love yourself inside and out!**
   Bianca was in love with her self on the outside - conceit, but not in love with herself on the inside.

2. **Learn to let go!**
   Bianca held on to the relationship with Chauncey after he cheated on her and had a baby outside of their relationship.

3. **Have some standards! Don't degrade yourself for someone else!**
   Sarah took drugs and slept with her boyfriend and his brother just to be in a relationship.

4. **Never allow someone else to validate your self worth.**
   Cynthia felt she wasn't good enough for her fiance' and became anorexic and depressed because he was gay.

5. **Love yourself after the breakup!**
   Sarah, Bianca, and Cynthia all needed to learn to continue on with their lives after their breakups and saga stories. Keep yourself up and together.

6. **Know how to ask and require the love that you want!**
   Kyle set the standard for how he and Bianca's relationship started and ended.

7. **Keep a clean house! Surround yourself with people who love themselves and you!**
   Bianca moved out of the apartment and back home with her mom for support and love after Sarah's betrayal.

8. **Be with a man because he is a MAN, not just a man!**
   Sarah and Bianca both learned this lesson in that they both were in relationships with men just to say that they had someone.

9. **Allow a MAN to be a man!**
   Bianca had to step back some and allow Kyle to work through his problems with Tamara in hopes that he would make the right decisions. She offered support without hounding him to do what she wanted all of the time.

10. **Don't be afraid to say what you want out of a relationship!**
    Bianca learned this throughout the book, sort of likeher life lesson after she met Kyle and began to date him. She also got this experience through being a friend and going through thing with both of her girlfriends - commitment without an emphasis on sex drugs and lies.

ABOUT THE AUTHOR

Lydia M. Lacy was born and raised in Detroit, Michigan. She attended Cass Technical High School and graduated from Wayne State University with her Bachelors of Arts degree in Speech-Language Pathology in 1997. She later returned to Wayne State and earned her Master of Arts degree in the same field in 1999. She is an active member of the American Speech and Hearing Association and is currently working in the Detroit public school system as a teacher of the speech and language impaired. Mrs. Lacy resides in a small Michigan suburb with her husband and two children.